Recycled Lives

(The Seraphim Network - The Everyday Series, Book 3)

By Yasmin Hawken

Thanks for all the support over the years

C. Head

Copyright © 2019 by
Charlotte Head & Kay Hawken as Yasmin Hawken

All Rights Reserved

All characters and events in this publication, other than those clearly in the public domain, are fictitious and any resemblance to real persons, living or dead, is purely coincidental.

Cover Art by:
Anya Kelleye Designs

Edited by:
Lauralynn Elliott

Seraphim Network logo:
Daniel Buckley

Acknowledgements

We want to thank everyone who supports us, from those of you who purchase our books, to those who have helped us throughout the publication process. Without your continued support and belief, we could not keep creating this amazing world that we have to share with you all.

A special thank you goes to James, who originally brought the character of Jacques to life and allowed us to have our artistic way with him.

We hope you all enjoy the latest adventure, and we look forward to taking you on many more.

The Seraphim Network
Everyday Series

Recycled Lives

YasminHawken

Chapter One

The sun was threatening the horizon as Jacques came to halt in his chosen hiding place. Crouched behind the balustrade of a balcony, he looked down through a gap in the stylized posts to the ballroom below. It was an event of excess. People dressed in expensive clothing. Or a severe lack of. When body modification was as extensive as it was in Seattle, people liked to show off their enhanced bodies. Whether that was a few inches cut from the waist or anything from face reshaping to an unusual eye color or breast implants, cosmetic surgery was a fashion accessory. These sorts of people paraded around in outfits that covered the bare essentials but showed that they had money to become the 'perfect' versions of themselves.

Jacques hated these people. He was augmented himself, a set of blackmarket cybereyes that he was still paying off, but they were useful; he could enhance his vision, see body heat through walls or see perfectly in low light situations. When you were historically poor, it was hard to see the point of purchases of such excess, where the only goal seemed to be to show off how much cash you had to burn. He scanned the crowd using the vision enhancement on his cybereyes to locate his target—Lucy. His teammate. She strode through the crowds with confidence in a tight-fitting outfit that left nothing to the imagination. Her boyfriend, Zane, was a lucky man.

"Jacques, wanna give me a location here?" Lucy said, her murmured voice coming from his earbud.

He pulled back from the edge of the balcony and flicked through the camera feeds he had active on his AR. He wasn't a hacker, but when you had the technical know-how, getting access through the hardlined wires was simple.

"You're looking at the back left hand door next to the stage. Guy's holding a neon blue and black drink," Jacques said as he spotted their target in the corner of the room.

"And we're sure he has no eye augmetics?" she asked with a slight tone of concern in her voice.

"If he has, they aren't legal. We need to hurry; we have three minutes until sun up," he said. If they waited too long, their escape plan was screwed.

Communications went silent as Lucy approached the mark. He watched on the cameras as she played with her blonde ringlets, a flirty smile on her porcelain face. She reached out and placed a gentle touch on his hand; that was the signal.

With deft movements, he used his wire clippers to snip the main line to the room's lights. The huge ballroom was plunged into darkness. There were shrieks and gasps from the assembled guests. He glanced down, his cybernetics adapting to the small amount of dawn light by activating the low light vision modification. Lucy was nowhere to be seen. Hopefully that was a good thing.

Before anyone could trace the breach in the powerline back to him, he grabbed his tools and jumped to his feet. With the black body suit he wore, he would be indistinguishable from the darkened corridors. As a stealth specialist, the night and the shadows were his best friend.

"Jacques, where are you?" said Lucy's whispered hurried tone.

"On my way. Hold your shit," he said as he made quick but quiet progress through the upstairs corridor.

Third turning, second door, fourth window. Third turning, second door, fourth window.' He repeated the instructions over and over to himself. These large elegant houses were like mazes; how anyone lived in them he'd never know. He was just happy that his apartment had a separate living room and bedroom, let alone having three reception rooms, an ostentatious ballroom, a private parlor and twelve bedrooms.

The corridor was almost pitch black, so dark that even his low light systems were having issues with providing him clear visibility, and that made him uncomfortable. He was relieved when he reached the target door and threw it open. The room's curtains were opened to welcome in the weak morning light, which gave him full visibility. He was glad he had gone for the flare compensation adaption when getting his eyes done; it had stopped him getting suddenly blinded by sudden sensory input of the morning sunlight. He ran to the fourth window.

The window was alarmed as expected; the faint etchings of circuitry at the edges of each of the panes was a dead giveaway. Reaching into one of his hidden pockets, he extracted a small toolkit. It was a simple system. He expected people with this much money to have something a little more complex. He was almost disappointed by the lack of challenge presented to him. With the alarm system cut, he threw open the window and jumped out.

The wind cut through him as he fell, instantly chilling him. The body suit, while good for stealth, wasn't great at keeping him warm. The freefall was only three stories, but he could feel his heart pounding away in his chest. His instincts feared injury even though the logical side of him knew he'd been fine, and he truly enjoyed the feeling of nothing beneath his body

With a heavy thud, he hit the inflatable pad below, the impact causing his teeth to crack together. It would only take moments for the pad to deflate, and as soon as his partner joined him, they'd be on their way with no real signs they'd been here.

"Here, take your clothes," Lucy said from behind him. He turned to find the pretty blonde brandishing his equipment at him. She was already dressed in jeans and a thick jacket.

"You got it, right?" Jacques asked as he grabbed the clothes and pulled on the cargo pants.

"Of course," she said as she opened her palm and showed a beautiful high-priced wrist watch. Even though the devices were rarely used thanks to AR, they were a sign of money. He had no idea what the Network's interest in it was, but it was his and Lucy's job to get it. They didn't need to know why the Network wanted it.

He pulled on his winter jacket, and by the time he was done, Lucy had forced the blow-up pad back into its pack and was ready to leave. With that, they quickly made their way back to the street. The perfect time of day to make yourself disappear—rush hour. They stepped into the heavy foot traffic moving with the throngs of people until they reached the subway system.

The stench of piss and sweat was thick and unforgiving as they descended the well-used staircase. The cream tiled walls were littered with AR posters advertising a whole host of things. From job openings, to band performances, to people selling their bodies, and posters selling augmentations. You could find anything here, not that you would trust a lot of the things you found in the subway system. Jacques had been bitten by that once. Never again.

As they reached the ticket barrier, Jacques stopped and removed a small patch from his hand. The translucent patch covered and disrupted the signals from the chip implanted in his palm. Everything about a person was stored on the chip that was inserted straight after birth. A simple scan could produce your entire history: medical records, school records, employment records, every house you had ever lived in. It also held all your banking information and, of course, your current location.

Jacques placed his palm in the ticket scanner. A machine read his identity chip, and with his permission, deducted the subway fare from his bank account. The turnstile clicked, and he stepped into the hub of the subway system. Streams of people filtered through different doors, each person in a desperate rush to their destination. When you had to work multiple jobs just to keep a roof over your head, time was a precious, finite commodity that no one wanted to waste by traveling.

The different scents from the food outlets and the people, combined with the cacophony of noise and movement, was a real assault on the senses. He turned to see Lucy get shoved by a larger man in a bright red trench coat and neon blue hair. She turned to throw the man a glare as he continued unhindered on his route through the swarm of people.

"EXCUSE YOU," Lucy said loudly before straightening her jacket and turning to Jacques. "One of these days I'm going to invest in a car. I can't stand the fucking subway."

"Maybe you should move in with your boyfriend, then you could afford one," Jacques said with a knowing smirk. Lucy and Zane had been growing close for the last couple months, and he'd asked her to move in twice—into what was, in fact, her own house no less—but for some reason, she was hesitating.

"If you think it's such a great idea, why don't you move in with him?" Lucy said childishly.

"I would, but he hogs all the covers," Jacques responded sarcastically, his smile becoming mischievous and teasing as he looked at her.

Lucy huffed a little and started for the stairs to their station. Well, that was the end of that conversation. He shook his head and followed after her. Maybe one day he'd get her to talk about what was going on with her.

The small cramped corridors opened out into a much larger room. The subway platform was alive with throngs of humans waiting to force themselves into the large metal tubes. It was a good thing he wasn't claustrophobic; otherwise, he'd be screwed. With Lucy at his side, they pushed through to where they needed to be.

"Oh, god, I can't wait to get to bed," Lucy said with a yawn.

"You going home or to Zane's?" he asked.

"Probably home. It's closer to the office, and I don't want to be fighting Sawyer for the shower again," Lucy said with a chuckle. "What's your plan? Back to Venom's or off training?"

It had been nearly six weeks since he'd moved out of Venom's place, but he hadn't wanted to tell Lucy. There was no way he would escape without her asking questions. How did you tell your friend that you had to move out of your apartment because of an ungodly unrequited crush on your flatmate, who was now in a committed relationship with someone else? There was no way he'd ever live it down.

"I'm gonna grab a drink then go home," Jacques responded. He'd specifically used the term home and not Venom's, so technically then he wasn't lying. He felt the looming threat of how hurt she would be when she found out he had hidden this from her, but he forced it down. She wasn't willing to talk about her shit with Zane, and he wasn't willing to talk about his shit with Venom. That made them even in his eyes.

There was a rumbling that echoed around the room as a subway car came thundering into the station and a screeching of brakes as it came to a halt. As soon as the doors opened, people started moving. They boarded the train along with the hundreds of other people and made basic conversation as the train thundered through the tunnels beneath the city.

Chapter Two

Ava came awake suddenly, her hand instantly gripping the gun that was stashed under her pillow. Her eyes darted around the darkened room until she picked up the edges of the beaten furniture that decorated the place she now called home. When she found nothing threatening in the room, she convinced her heart that it could slow down. Suddenly, there was a knocking on the door. That's what had woken her. She slid from beneath the covers and made for the door. She opened it just a crack to see Hamish standing on the other side.

"This is your wake-up call, love," Hamish said in his friendly but gruff voice.

The tenseness rolled off her shoulders in that moment. Even after weeks of this ritual, hearing the knock at her door was still enough to shake her. If she woke to the sound of someone else too close to her in her old place then a fight was about to take place. With a yawn, she dragged her hand down over her face.

"Thanks, Hamish," she said, expecting him to turn away and head back into the bar.

"Y'know that gauntlet I brought you can act as an alarm, right?" Hamish said with a raised eyebrow.

"Yeah, I just need the extra boot up my ass," she lied. Hamish nodded and made his way back down the corridor. He didn't need to know that she had no idea how to work that technology of his.

Where she had grown up, the most advanced tech were things like vehicles and guns, nothing compared to the levels of tech in Seattle. The Fringe was a decrepit and backwards place. Existing in a walled off section of Seattle, The Fringe had been left to fester and decay. Gangs had risen, and the people had been forced to make do, or they starved or died of infection. If you wanted anything good, you had to pray that you had something extraordinarily valuable to barter with Big Boss, the ruthless ganger that ruled the roost.

When Jacques, Lucy, and Zane had entered her home in the trash heaps of The Fringe, she hadn't thought much of them. They had wanted information, and for that, they had brought her with them to the bright lights of Seattle. It had been difficult trying to acclimatize to the world on this side of the wall. The fact that the city never slept had been the greatest shock; even at night, the neon lights illuminated the cityscape like a sunrise. She found she missed the quiet, pitch darkness that accompanied nighttime in The Fringe. Then there was the tech. It had taken her close to a month to get used to the payment system in the bar and paying for her own goods when she went shopping, let alone tackling the messaging and social media systems that everyone seemed to insist on using. She felt so lost, but she would never tell anyone that. Her hard front was what protected her from being exploited by others. That's what she had been taught, and keeping her struggles to herself had served her well so far.

Using the small sink in her room, she strip washed before dressing in her attire for the day, a red, cold shoulder cut blouse with low V neckline and a pair of dark navy low-rise jeans that she had stitched some additional embellishments into the back pockets of. It was simpler than her old style of dress and only showed a little skin. She was past the days of selling her body, but in the bar, showing a little cleavage was enough to get the patrons tipping. Sex sold in The Fringe, and apparently Seattle was no different.

Since she'd settled here, she had been forced to think about what she was going to do with her life. She had been raised to be a whore, but now she could do whatever she wanted, and in a way that scared her. Hamish had seen she was set up with what she needed: fake ID, bank account, and all the tech. He'd even bought her some simple clothing as she'd only had the clothes on her back, and they were only fit to be burnt. To pay him back, she worked most nights behind the bar for reduced pay. It worked for her; she got a place to stay, was able to learn the new world she found herself in, and the job was easy, but it wasn't what she wanted to do with her life.

In the Valkyries, her path had been clear. Do her time of service, show her potential as a leader, and rise the ranks to head up her own piece of the territory, maybe even the whole gang. No more taking orders from anyone. She would be her own woman. But after her expulsion from their ranks, those dreams had died, and her only focus had become survival. Now she needed a new dream. She still wanted to be her own boss, but she had no idea what she could sell this side of the wall other than sex.

"Delivery day today," Hamish said as she stepped into the bar.

The best day of week. She grabbed a band and pulled her long blonde hair into a ponytail. Nothing like carrying a shit ton of heavy crates from the landing dock through to the store room while two guys flirted with her. She was quick to remind herself that it was better than having to fight them for their wares or be forced into bed with them. She was good at sex and enjoyed it when it was on her terms, but being told who to sleep with or what she had to do to them had grated on every fiber of her being. It's how she had ended up bedding Big Boss. When he came looking for a new girl, she made him want to take her home. Sure, he was a little crazy, but he looked okay and gave her more freedom than a usual Valkyrie, and she had chosen him. He just didn't know it.

"I'll get on it," Ava said with a nod to Hamish. The older man smiled back at her.

"Be careful; don't hurt yourself," Hamish said. The people at the Oaken Casket were like a little family. Hamish genuinely seemed to care about the staff and the regulars like they were his children. It was something she hadn't really seen before now, and the whole thing made her a little awkward.

"I won't," she said as she headed into the backroom, trying to shake off the uncomfortable feeling. She needed to save up as much money as she could to move out and start her business, whatever it was going to be. She had to put herself first like always. No emotional attachments. They just held you back and got you in trouble. She pushed the thought to the back of her head and started stacking the old boxes.

*****

Once they'd had their meeting in the office, Jacques and Lucy made their way back into the sweaty subway station. The buses were cheaper, but the subways were faster. Right now, they had the cash to be able to put speed before price. They separated just after the barriers as Lucy was heading to a different part of town. It allowed Jacques a brief moment of alone time. Well, he wasn't truly alone; the subway car was filled with people, but no one attempted to interact with him.

When he reached his stop, he made his way from the small station to the streets above. The fresh air was a relief. The worst of the cold weather was over, and the days were getting longer. Spring was definitely here. He shoved his hands in his jacket and made his way down the street.

This area of town was very different from the place he'd come from on this morning's job with Lucy.

Yasmin Hawken

The richer part of town was well kept. Clean lawns, uncluttered streets, and regular members of the City Security. But not here. Graffiti decorated the tenement buildings, while the scent of trash stuck in your nose. A lot of the city services didn't seem to stretch this far, and the last bastion of greenery was six blocks back for God's sake. And yet, somehow Jacques felt a lot more at home here.

He headed down a set of steps to a basement door with two large armored men on either side—mercenaries hired to keep the place safe. There was no signage; the people who came here knew exactly where they were going. He pushed the door open and stepped inside. The bar was decorated in dark colors, no doubt a trick to stop them having to worry about any stubborn stains that wouldn't go away no matter how hard you scrubbed them. The bar beyond could be considered dark and dingy, but to him, there was nowhere more homey. The back room to this place had actually been his home for a little while. The Oaken Casket was one of a kind. The bar was a place for mercenaries to meet and find jobs. It was a home for the more unsavory folk, but the staff and the regulars knew each other as well as such a secretive lot could and looked after one another. It was the unwritten code of the place.

As he approached the bar, a man stepped up, wiping a glass with a questionable looking rag. He was an older man; the creases and calluses showed his age. His square jaw was home to an impressive silver beard, and his dark eyes were aware of everyone who came into his bar. His name was Hamish, and for the longest time, he'd been like a father to Jacques. He picked him up when he fell and always tried to stop him making stupid decisions. That wasn't always easy.

"Evening, boy. How are you?" Hamish said. He reached under the bar, took a glass, poured a pint, and placed it in front of Jacques. The beauty of being a regular was that you didn't need to place your order.

"I'm good, old man. What's news?" Jacques asked, bringing the drink to his lips and sipping from it.

"Oh, you know, the usual. Had a scuffle in here at lunch time. M.A.X took issue with the bad attitude of some new blood ex jar-heads who came in spoiling for a fight." Far from concerned, Hamish's voice showed how much he had been amused that a fight had broken out in his bar.

"I assume M.A.X put them in their place," Jacques said, a grin spreading across his face as he glanced over at M.A.X's preferred table. He looked a little more rough around the edges than usual, but aside from a split lip, bruised knuckles, and a black eye, didn't seem to have come off too badly from his altercation. The short-tempered man was as old as dirt, mad as a hatter, and practically part of the furniture of the Oaken Casket. He was anything but frail and didn't suffer fools gladly. Or at all, really.

"Course he did. Didn't even have time to tell the little pricks to fuck off before M.A.X decided to break a pool stick over the leader's head to shut his hole." Hamish chuckled.

Hamish launched into a blow by blow account of the fight that Jacques was sure was embellished by the older man to make it sound more exciting than it had been. He didn't mind. He liked the way Hamish spoke; the familiarity of his particular brand of storytelling relaxed him after his long day. The tale he wove was one of violence and bloodshed incited by brash words from a newcomer who clearly didn't know the lay of the land and was used to being the toughest guy. It was the same as pretty much any story that took place here. When you catered for the unsavory types, trouble tended to come your way. Not that it ever seemed to bother Hamish. So long as his patrons stopped short of killing each other on his property and paid for anything that they broke that wasn't covered by their medical insurance. Jacques settled in the stool, enjoying the sound of Hamish waffling and the familiar bustle of the rowdy patrons the Casket attracted. He wasn't quite ready to go home to his empty apartment right now. Maybe a couple of drinks would help with that.

*****

With a sigh of relief, Ava placed the final crate of beer on to the stack. The weekly delivery was always a big one, and the regular streams of people definitely knew how to put the drink away. She grabbed a bottle of water and took a swig before regarding the stock before her. It was going to be a busy and laborious day as she sorted all the bottles and kegs into their places. It was better than where she had been, so much better than selling her body for a cheap high and a roof over her head. She glanced out into the bar. The dark and dingy place had started to become her home; it was so much nicer than anywhere she had lived before. Even the main Valkyrie house seemed like squalor compared to here.

It was time for a break. Ava leaned against the wall and looked out into the bar. She watched from the backroom as Jacques made his way into the Oaken Casket and settled at his usual place at the bar. It had become a regular occurrence. At least three times a week he'd come in, settle in his bar stool, and make basic conversation with Hamish before nursing a drink or two for a couple hours. He hadn't noticed her, though. She wasn't sure he even knew that she still stayed here, not that it bothered her either way.

He looked different from the last time she had seen him. His usually clean-shaven face showed signs of a five o'clock shadow, while his eyes focused entirely on the drink in front of him. He swirled the liquid in the bottom of the glass, watching it intently. There was obviously something on his mind.

It had been a few months since their escape from The Fringe. The gang infested hellhole was just a thing of nightmares now. A regular nightmare that visited her every night and left her cold and sweating in her bed. Jacques had been part of the team that had helped bring her from that God forbidden hole out into the world proper, and that was one of the reasons that she avoided him. She was thankful for what he and his team had done for her, but to admit to him and the others how grateful she was seemed somewhat weak in her eyes. Even so, his status as one of the few people she knew of this side of the wall meant that she had felt the draw to talk to him a few times. She supposed it was time to stop hiding away and bite the bullet. It wasn't in her nature to be such a coward. She picked up a box of beer and made her way into the bar.

"Do you actually have a home to go to? You seem to prop up this bar better than the supports," she asked as she placed the box down and started loading the beers into the mini fridges.

"Yeah, I got a place. It's like a palace. Four walls, hot water, power, a view of the city, and it even has a bed that doesn't squeak like it's about to fall out from under you," he said with a slight smirk.

"Wow, look at you. Mr Made of Money. Don't forget to tip your server," she said with a wink. She grabbed him a shot glass and poured a measure of whiskey. "So why are you here and not there?"

"I'm here for the enchanting atmosphere and this," he said. He raised the glass to his lips and peered at her over the slight foam. He held his eye contact as he took a long sip. He smacked his lips as he placed the drink back on the bar. "Ah, that's good. A damn sight better than wandering the streets."

"What? These lovely streets? With the beautiful sights, smells, and the friendly locals," she said acerbically. She didn't really feel that way. This place was a major upgrade from where she had lived before, but it wasn't idyllic. The streets were still grime covered and the residents as desperate and oppressed as her home. They just had access to running water, healthcare, and technological escapes from reality. Hamish had drilled it into her that she needed to keep her origins under wraps. She had to appear like a local to not arouse suspicion. If Seattle Security found out she had come from The Fringe, she'd be sent right back into that pit.

"Already fancying some elevation from your current situation? They aren't *that* bad," he said with a sarcastic smile, spinning idly on his bar stool. "I used to be one of those beautiful sights, smells, and friendly locals."

She wasn't entirely sure if Jacques was flirting with her or just being ignorant. Throughout her life, her interaction with men had only ever boiled down to one thing that they wanted from her. Her upbringing had reinforced the notion, making it clear that she only had one purpose in life—sex for profit to help fund the gang. She didn't know or really understand any other way. She was still trying to learn the way things worked this side of the wall, and Jacque's signals confused her.

"My current situation is a dream come true compared to my last one. Y'know living in a trash heap was just greeeeaat," she said, sarcasm dripping heavily from her tone. When she had been exiled from the Valkyries, she had been forced to live amongst the trash on the outskirts of the gang territories, struggling to survive. "The rats were the worst part of it. Waking up to them in my bed. Though that at least meant I would have breakfast that day."

"You had a bed? You were lucky, princess; I had to sleep on my rats," he said, that smirk still firmly in place. She was still trying to figure out if he was joking or not. Did he really think his life had been harder than hers?

"Well, it wasn't really a bed, more moldy blankets on the floor. That's totally the same thing," she said. Just thinking about that trash heap sent a cold shiver up her spine. It had taken weeks to wash the musty scent of stale mold out of her skin and hair. She never wanted to be anywhere like that again.

"Blankets, too? Luxury. You've clearly never slept in a dumpster you had to steal from another hobo," he said with a playful grin. She shook her head a little; the Seattle born man really thought his bad fortune could compare to that of her Fringe background.

"A dumpster? Man, I was doing that when I was ten. I had to fight a girl to have a dumpster with a lid; when I won, I pushed her into the shit pit…literally exactly what it sounds like…a pit full of shit," she said. It had been almost three months since she'd escaped The Fringe, and she couldn't imagine going back. She had quickly come to love things like indoor plumbing and living in a house that didn't get soggy when it rained.

"You fight dirty, for real. I like that," he said, taking a contemplative gulp from his beer. "Once I broke into a house while the occupants were at work just to take a shower. While I was there, I decided they didn't need their abundant collection of shower gels and soap…or toilet paper."

"I did something similar. One of the last johns I had was a real piece of work, so while he was sorting himself out, I stole the rounds from his pistol. Those things fetch a fair price at the market," Ava explained.

Recycled Lives

She didn't add the part that she never saw him again; no doubt he started a fight and got shot up because of his empty gun. In The Fringe, you had to protect yourself.

"I used to practice my pickpocketing by stealing things out of people's shopping carts. When I'd get caught, I used to pretend that there was something wrong with me. Sometimes they would be sympathetic enough to buy the goods for me," he said with a slight chuckle.

On this side of the wall, the rules were different, but it was nice to meet someone who hadn't had a good upbringing. It made her feel a lot more normal.

"When I was young, I used to break into the kitchens of the Valkyrie kids' dorms to steal the sweet treats they had there. They didn't let us have any to…y'know to keep us skinny. When they noticed things were missing, I was good at shifting the blame onto some of the others. I never got caught for it," she said. She hated to think about those dorms. Ten beds to a room, ten little girls who either grew to embrace the Valkyrie lifestyle or were kicked out to find their place elsewhere.

"Is that so? Well, buckle up, sister, as this one can't be beaten," he said with a wicked grin as he set his pint back on the bar. "In my fourth and final orphanage, there was this hard-ass drill sergeant of a carer who threatened to starve us if we didn't comply with his rules. All us orphans hated him, so I got two of them to beat me black and blue. I filed abuse charges against him, and the others testified as witnesses. He's still in jail now, and will be for a few more years."

There was a little part of her that was impressed at his dedication to help people, or was it revenge in this case? Either way, he had been willing to go the distance and take a beating to put a bad guy behind bars. She found herself respecting him for that. It had been something she'd been forced to do herself.

"I killed a guy once. He was screwing with a few of the young girls. The Valkyries start preparing the girls for the trade when they're fifteen. When I was eighteen, there was this guy, and he was beating on some of the younger girls if they didn't do things 'right' the first time. I mean that he was nearly killing them. I only intended to castrate the bastard, y'know make him pay, but I didn't expect the blood loss," she said.

She remembered that day well. Yes, the Valkyries sold sex, but they usually looked after the girls in their care. Most were their daughters. When the new guard had come in, she hadn't thought much of him, just another gangster with an ego complex. When he started knocking the girls around, she had told someone, but no one seemed too concerned. She knew she had to step in. Death wasn't a scary thing in The Fringe; you saw it most days. But when it was by your own hand, things just seemed so different. Until that day, she had hurt people, but had never taken another life.

"At least he deserved it," Jacques said with a sigh. Ava looked back to him. All the humor of their banter had evaporated. The lines of his face hardened due to whatever he was thinking. "I'd wager a lot of people here have taken a life, and hopefully, those who died also deserved it. Maybe someone here once came home to find a stranger in his girlfriend's bed and assumed the worst. Took it too far…and…"

He trailed off. His eyes stared unblinkingly at the back wall. Whatever happened had obviously fucked him up. It was easy for her to forget that death and murder wasn't a part of everyday life here like it had been for her. She grabbed a bottle of liquor from the bar, filling two glasses and placing one in front of him.

"We all do things that we live to regret. Sometimes for good reason and sometimes not. At the end of the day, it's what shapes us. I was trained to be a whore and nothing else. What's truly going to shape me is what happens this side of the wall," she said, and she drank the whole shot. It burned all the way down, but that was a feeling she liked.

"I don't like the shape that it made me…nor the others involved," he said slightly gruffly. He downed the shot and slid the glass back to her. "So you've settled in nicely it seems. Anything else you need?" Ava noted the deliberate change of topic and allowed it. The man clearly wasn't any keener on discussing his past life than she was on reliving hers.

"Hamish is making sure I get what I need. Not that I understand the shit he's giving me. It took me three or four weeks just getting used to the fucking payment system," she said with a chuckle as she tried to brush off her insecurity. She topped up her own glass and returned the bottle to the stand.

"I'm surprised that fossil knows how to log into his own gauntlet. I've wasted most of my life living through mine," Jacques said, seeming to cheer up at the conversation change. He grabbed a peanut from the nearby bowl and flicked it with perfect aim to land straight between her cleavage. "I guess I could fill the position of strict and overbearing sensei if you fancy being an adoring and insatiably grateful student."

"So you want a woman who will fawn over you and tell you that you are wonderful. Is that it, Jacques?" she asked with a coy smirk as she fished the peanut from her cleavage and flicked it back at him.

"Who wouldn't? But if you do, well, the…uh…praise would be returned," Jacques responded with a slight smirk. She leaned forward with her elbows on the bar.

"You assume I'm a girl who lives for praise," she said in a flirtatious tone that dripped with lust. It was a tone that she had perfected over the years. "Tell me where, and I'll be there."

His eyes focused on hers at the moment. She wondered how hard he was trying to not look at her breasts. Her shirt was stretched tightly over them, giving him a good view as she leaned forward. He turned his attention to the band on his wrist and typed something into his gauntlet. There was a beeping from her own wrist.

"You got that? We can start when you get off shift tomorrow if you like. Gives me a chance to spruce my place up a bit. Light some incense, delete my browsing history, hide the bodies. Real gentlemanly stuff," he said with a slight smirk.

"Aww, not hiding all the good stuff on my behalf, are you? Bodies make a fantastic centerpiece, don't you think?" she said with a slight laugh as she finished her drink and put the glass in the dishwasher. "Anyway, I better get back to work. I have to earn my keep around here. Have a good one."

With that, she turned back to the bar and set about stacking the beers in the fridge. She swore she could feel eyes watching her; she swore it was Jacques. When she turned around, she found the barstool empty, but his empty beer bottle stood solitary, and a generous tip waited to be transferred to her. It had been nice to have an actual conversation with someone for the first time in a long time.

Chapter Three

Lucinda always felt a buzz when she finished a job. The heady combination of adrenaline, pride, and the sense of accomplishment fueled her growing ambition to succeed and rise through the ranks. She felt like nothing would be out of her reach. The second she stepped foot into her bedroom at her shared house, the feeling evaporated, leaving her empty and deflated. It was like a cold breeze on warm skin—unwanted. She sighed and dumped her work pack on a chair. When she had picked this place, she had loved it. It was comfortable, spacious, the rent was good, and the area was safe enough she could leave her front door without being mugged. Now it just seemed cold and lifeless. A plain room to exist in, not a place to live.

She dropped herself on the bed and stared at the ceiling. Images floated on the ceiling projected from her AR. It was mainly pictures of her and Zane. God, that just made her miss him even more. They had only been dating for three months, but she already couldn't imagine her life without him.

When they had first met, she had been on the most dangerous job of her life. Sent into The Fringe, a walled-off hive of lawless gangs in the heart of the city, with Zane as their guide and only hope to navigate the treacherous landscape of decaying buildings and murderous locals. At first, she hadn't really liked him; he had come across as an arrogant, overconfident punk. It hadn't taken long for her to see that beneath the surface, he had a heart of gold. When his parents had died, he'd been left taking care of his five younger siblings, and he'd given up a lot, including one of his legs, to keep them safe. It was one of the things she loved most about him, but it also was one of her biggest worries. She never knew how far he would go if something happened to one of them, and the idea of having a boyfriend in prison frightened her.

Almost all of the family had spent all but the last year of their lives growing up in The Fringe. Therefore, they had been raised with a different moral code as well as different social and cultural norms from the rest of the residents of Seattle. That made things very difficult sometimes. Vincent and Ryker, the twins, were constantly getting into fist fights at school over the tiniest of slights, Sawyer would help herself to things without asking, Blair wouldn't take no for an answer, and Caspian had a major problem with authority. The six of them had their way of working through things, and she worried about how she was going to fit in with the situation. Not only were there the children, but there was also Dare, a young man that Zane had adopted and treated like family. Seven large, dysfunctional personalities who came from The Fringe. How did she fit in with that?

When Zane had initially asked her to move in with him a couple weeks ago, the idea had excited her, but then she had started to really think about it. She and Zane had only been dating for three months. It had been an amazing three months, but she was still scared things would go wrong, and if they did, what would she do then? He was currently living in the house she inherited from her parents as she'd suggested. She didn't want something to go wrong and have the awkward situation of what happened to the house or having to find herself a new place to live.

There was a gentle chiming from her gauntlet indicating a new message. It was from Zane. Almost as if he knew that she was stressing herself out about him. She started typing a response when she changed her mind and hit the video call button. The call was answered immediately. She was greeted by the beautiful sight of her muscled boyfriend. He was lying in his bed, the cream sheets covering his waist leaving his bare, muscled chest on show. His long sandy-brown hair partially covered his face. She found herself wanting to lean in and brush it out of the way just to look at him properly.

"Morning, Luce," he said with a tired yawn. The sun was rising, and it was time for both of them to be going to sleep. They both lived the night cycle, waking up just as evening would fall and going to sleep around dawn.

"Morning. Did you have a good night?" she asked, moving the call window to the AR wall above the bed so she could start getting herself ready for bed.

"Yeah, it was alright. Was hoping I'd get to see you, though," he said. Her heart expanded a little at his words. It was such a nice feeling to have someone who wanted to see her, yet here she was avoiding him.

"Sorry, after we'd been to the office, I couldn't face the trip back across town," she lied. She wasn't that tired; she just couldn't face him. She was scared he'd ask her to move in again, and she'd have to come up with some excuse, some reason as to why now wasn't a good time.

"That's fine. How did the job go? You were safe, right?" he asked.

"Yeah, don't worry. If anyone had come for me, I would have just used the moves you taught me," she said with a slight smile. When they had first met, she had been a lot weaker and could barely look after herself. Zane had made sure that changed. He worked for the Network as a Self Defense Instructor and didn't mind taking her on as his private student. As a result, her combat skills had improved dramatically as had her confidence.

"Good. Are you free tomorrow? I've got the day off as I've a meeting at the twins' school, but I'm free from one am. Maybe we could do something?" he asked. She was quiet for a moment as she tried to come up with an answer. "Luce, what's going on? You're being so distant."

"Nothing. I'm fine," she said too quickly for it to even seem true. She was great at talking to people, but with him, she just seemed to have some sort of weakness. She had since she met him. She was worried opening up her fears about moving in would upset him, and she really didn't want to have that fight with him. "I'll...uhh...get back to you about tomorrow. I have some things to do."

"Oh...okay. Well, I need to sleep. I'm here if you're free. Sleep well," he said, and he ended the call.

She stared at the dark ceiling where his image had been a few seconds ago. Why couldn't she be honest with him? Why couldn't she just say she wasn't ready? Until they'd met, Zane had never dated. Dating wasn't really a thing in The Fringe, and the transition to Seattle hadn't made it any easier to find someone. He'd confided in her how hard he found the difference in social norms this side of the wall, and she didn't want to hurt him.

She sat up again and looked around the room. There was still stuff in boxes from when she'd moved in, and she'd never seemed to have the time to unpack them. Maybe she had never been as settled here as she thought. She needed to figure out what she was going to do tonight, and no matter what she decided, she would go and see him, and they could talk. It wasn't like he'd end it if she wasn't ready to move in. Would he?

*****

Jacques looked around the small apartment he now called home. With a satisfied nod to himself, he went to the kitchen and turned on the coffee machine.

With the knowledge that Ava was coming around tonight, he had spent the evening tidying up. He didn't even know why he cared; he had just felt the need to make sure the place was presentable. Well, at least it was done now, and it would be at least a month before he felt the need to clean again.

He hadn't even managed to make a cup of coffee when there was a knock on the door. He knew exactly who it was; no one else had any idea where he lived these days. As he pulled the door open, he was greeted with the sight of Ava. Figure hugging hipster jeans, a white tank top, and a fitted denim jacket framed her tight body. Her long, wavy, blonde hair fell like waterfalls over her shoulders.

"So this is home? I'm disappointed; it looks almost normal," she said with a slight smirk. She stepped through the door and shrugged her jacket off her shoulders.

"What's normal?" he asked with a chuckle. He closed the door and went back to the coffee maker to finish the drinks.

"This," she said, indicating around the room. "I was expecting a man cave, maybe a skull fortress, or at least some nude woman on the AR wallpaper."

"A skull fortress? Okay... Ah, I just remembered," he said as he tapped on the gauntlet, making an incense diffuser smoke on the coffee table from a few taps of a button. He took two cups of coffee from the side and handed one to her, "Now where do you think we should begin?"

"How to work this useless strip would be great," she said, indicating the gauntlet on her wrist before she dropped herself into a seat at the two-person dining table.

Jacques had been using the AR Gauntlet for years; he couldn't even imagine how someone wouldn't know how to use it. A simple flick of the wrist, and an AR screen would pop up, allowing you access to so many features. His entire world evolved around it, his messaging, his calls, his calendar, his alarms, his bank details. Everything came from the simple black band.

"Alrighty, I'm going have you mastering that in no time," he said as he sat down at the table next to her.

Surprisingly, Ava was a very good student. With the brash attitude she portrayed, he had expected her to fight him, or not listen, but every time he looked to her, he had her full attention. She sat there and listened, asking questions at the right points. After an hour of instruction, she was managing most of the basic functions, and she received the praise he had promised.

"Okay, so this isn't as complicated as I thought," Ava said, with an almost childlike look of glee on her face as she flicked her wrist to bring up the AR menu. She had clearly been trying to hide how she really felt about the inability to understand the technology and was too afraid to ask for the help she needed. Her staunchly independent attitude was a throwback to her life in The Fringe, where it was take care of yourself or die. There was never any help to be found on the other side of the wall, not unless you had something of value to trade, and any sign of weakness was going to get you killed.

Jacques felt an unusual pride as he watched her interacting with the gauntlet. He felt that, for the briefest instant, he was getting an insight to what she could have been like if it wasn't for her rough upbringing.

"What do you want for this?" Ava asked abruptly.

"You think we are done? This was just the first lesson, and these were just the basics," Jacques said with a chuckle. There was so much more to tech that he had to teach her if she was going to pass as a Seattle native.

"Yeah, I know, but how much do you want for this lesson?" she asked.

"Nothing. I don't want anything," he said. He had done this because, well, he wasn't sure why, but he sure knew he didn't want payment for it. The look she gave him said she wasn't going to take no for an answer. "How about a drink? Somewhere other than the Casket."

She looked a little taken aback for a moment. Like the idea of going for a drink was infinitely more intimate than being invited into someone's home. He wasn't even sure why he'd suggested it, but he really wanted to get to know her a little better. When she didn't answer immediately, he started to work on a way to make it into a joke and shrug off the awkward atmosphere developing between them.

"Sure. Just give me a message when and where," she said. She pushed herself to her feet and grabbed her coat. "Now that I know how to send messages, it will make life a whole lot easier."

He liked the way she smiled at her accomplishment, and her enthusiasm was infectious. What he'd taught her today most children knew how to do, but she looked like she had accomplished something that was a huge deal. He supposed for her, it was. It was amazing to see how such a simple thing had evoked such a strong emotion in her. He couldn't wait to see her for more lessons and show her more of the world.

"I better head out. I have an early shift, so I need to get some sleep," Ava said over her shoulder as she headed for the door. "Thanks again. I'll see you soon."

He showed her out the door and watched as she walked down the corridor, almost disappointed that the corridor wasn't longer. When she had turned into the stairwell, he closed the door and locked himself inside his flat. He couldn't understand what was going on in his head at the moment. A quick, cold, shower, and then he would get some sleep himself. Maybe things would be made clear in the morning.

Chapter Four

It had been a couple of days since Lucinda had spoken with Zane, and she felt guilty as hell not spending his day off with him, but she had needed some time to herself to sort her head out. Their romance had been such a passionate whirlwind that she needed to be away from him just to figure out how she felt about everything—how she felt about their future. It hadn't been until she worked through it properly, and contemplated the hypothetical possibility of life without him and his family, that she'd realized exactly how much he meant to her, and how much she wasn't willing to risk losing him. He was moving fast for Seattle standards, which was a cultural difference that had shocked her into uncertainty, but he was also loyal, fiercely protective, and made her feel things that she knew she would be hard pressed to find again if she were foolish enough to let him slip through her fingers.

That sickening feeling when she considered not having him as part of her life was all she needed to make her next step clear. She packed herself a few things and made for his place, with a stop at Tayvian's bakery on the way to buy some sweet treats for the family.

As she reached the townhouse, she couldn't help the smile. Once this had been her family home, before her parents had disappeared when she was a child. At twenty-one she had inherited what was left of their estate. At first, she could barely bring herself to step inside the place. It was like a mausoleum with everything exactly the same as the day her parents went missing, only covered in dusty dust sheets. She had allowed Zane and his siblings to live in the place rent free. Originally, the seven of them had been living in a small three bed house, and it had been very cramped. She had also hoped they would make a mark on the house and bring it back to life, so maybe one day she could walk in without feeling intense sorrow. They had certainly made their mark.

In the days after she'd handed over the keys, Zane had carefully packed up everything in the house and moved it to a storage facility. She'd asked him to just get rid of it as she couldn't bear the thought of sorting through everything, but he had refused. He'd said she'd regret it someday, and she suspected he was right. After that, they had re-painted the place and outfitted it with new furniture. Zane, Caspian, and Dare had spent a week working their asses off to get the place decorated. When Lucinda had stepped back in it again, she couldn't believe what she was looking at. It was so sleek and modern, just so different, which was exactly what she had wanted for the place.

Recycled Lives

"Good morning," she called out as she stepped through the front door into the large open plan living room/dining room/kitchen combination. There was a mixture of greetings from the family members gathered in the dining room. She placed the small box she'd brought with her onto a side table and made for dining room area.

Vincent, Ryker, Sawyer, and Blair were sitting at the table with Zane standing watch by one of the kitchen sides. The four kids were all working on what looked like homework on their AR devices. Zane hadn't had much of an education in The Fringe, so he was adamant that the kids would have a better start in life than he'd had. Every day after school, they had to sit at the table and get their work done before they were allowed to play. Zane insisted on it, and most of the time the kids complied. Lucinda was glad she had missed the first few months of Zane implementing the rule. His stories of all the tricks and tantrums the kids had thrown to try to escape doing their work sounded exhausting.

Their rough starts in The Fringe could easily be seen in their behavior. Zane was trying to smooth the roughest traits out of them, but sometimes the thug in all of them came out. Only a year and a half in civilized society hadn't fully erased what they had been, but they were definitely making improvements.

"Morning, love," Zane said as his hand snaked around her waist and pulled her against him. He leaned in, pressing his lips against hers in a demanding kiss. The feeling of his kisses always lit a fire in her. When she heard a girly giggle from the table, she pulled back to see Blair giggling at them from behind her tiny hands.

"Haven't you got work to do?" Lucinda said with a questioning smile to Blair. Blair quickly put her head down and carried on working.

Lucinda turned her attention back to Zane. His sandy-brown hair was damp and pulled back into a ponytail, and a clean but musky scent clung to him, which meant he'd just taken a shower after work. She wished she had been here to join him. Running wet and soapy hands over that muscled body made her day.

"How was your day?" Zane asked as he went back to the stove and stirred the huge pot that was on the heat.

"It was okay, nothing much to report. What about yours?" she asked, coming up to his side and looking into the pot. It was filled with meatballs and marinara sauce, and the aromatic scent caused a rumble in her stomach. Zane's cooking ability was still limited to packeted meat and sauce from a jar, but he was beginning to experiment with flavor packets and powders.

"Standard day at the training room, really," Zane said as he went about dishing up the food. "You eating with us?"

"Yes, please. I even bought dessert for afterwards," she said with a smile as she gestured to the Tayvian's box on the kitchen side. Even she was excited for the sweet pastries, despite having had one for breakfast.

Recycled Lives

While Zane was focused on serving dinner, Lucinda headed to the dining table to help the kids with homework. It had quickly become one of their rituals. Lucinda had access to an education which Zane never had, which meant he struggled to help the kids with any schoolwork related issues. She was more than happy to help the kids out and actually really enjoyed playing teacher. His little family was quickly becoming hers, too, which she both loved and was terrified by. After losing one family and spending years with no one to call her own, suddenly being a part of someone else's was a little unnerving.

"...So, yeah, when she looked at me, she wasn't going to say no," Caspian said arrogantly as he entered the kitchen with Dare.

Lucinda looked up from the table to see the final sibling entering the room. Caspian was the second eldest, and he was the spitting image of his older brother. The same sandy hair, the same jawline, the same eyes, but most of all, the same hot-headed temperament. The two brothers came to blows a lot. She hadn't witnessed a fight between the boys before, just the aftermath of black eyes and broken end tables. It had been the usual way of things in The Fringe; disagreements had been solved with fists rather than words. Zane had pretty much managed to step out of The Fringe way of life, but Caspian just had that way of pushing him too far—too much male testosterone.

"Hey, Luce," Caspian said, giving her a brief one-armed hug and a peck on the cheek. The guy may be an arrogant show off, but he had always been good to her.

"Wanna grab the plates, Cas?" Zane said, pointing to the cupboard with the stirring spoon.

"No problem," Cas said, heading straight for the cupboard and doing as asked.

Dare leaned on the side next to her. He wasn't a blood relation of the family but had been taken in as an honorary brother long ago. When the family had escaped The Fringe, Dare had accidently been left behind. On the mission when Lucinda had met Zane, they had brought Dare with him. It had been interesting watching the young man try to acclimatize to the city.

"Hey, Dare, how's it going?" Lucinda asked as the young man gave her a beaming smile.

"I'm doing good, thanks. Zane's talking about getting me a tutor to learn stuff. Not sure how I feel about that," Dare said with a look of concern. In The Fringe, he would have been taught what he needed to survive and fight; reading and writing were not core subjects.

"You're a smart guy; you'll rock it," she said, giving him a smile that she hoped would convey a little confidence to him.

"Thanks, Lucy," he said with a smile, and he settled at the table beside the twins. He looked over their shoulders at the AR they worked on. There was a smile on his face but concern in his eyes. She couldn't imagine how hard it would be to go from a technology void world like The Fringe to Seattle where almost every day to day task involved using one device or another. They were an amazing little family, and she was determined to help them as much as she could.

Recycled Lives

There was a clattering of plates, which got her attention, and the scent of the food seemed to grow stronger. Lucinda looked back to see plates of food being dished out. She felt her stomach growl painfully, the meaty scent was so enticing. Unsurprisingly, the kids suddenly weren't even remotely interested in homework. Lucinda had learned quickly that as soon as food was in the picture, the kids couldn't focus on anything else. After spending the time in The Fringe and seeing the food they had grown up on, she couldn't blame them. A hearty meal had been a rare treat for them and would have also gained lots of attention from other residents looking to steal something hot and nourishing.

The meal was distributed, and there was no conversation, just the sounds of cutlery on china as the food was quickly demolished. Lucinda was always the last to finish; the kids ate like it was their last meal and all but licked their plates clean. It made her sad that it was so ingrained in them that even after a year, they were still obsessed with food. As soon as every crumb of the sweet pastries had been consumed, the kids went about clearing up after dinner. She smiled as she watched them working together. They had really had brought life back to her parents' old home.

Chapter Five

Ava saw the glowing sign that indicated she had arrived at her destination. Neon was supposed to be one of the most popular clubs in Seattle Central. Finding her way around was so much easier since Jacques had taught her how to use the map program on her gauntlet. The black building was decorated with what looked like neon paint splotches that periodically shifted around the blank canvas. The vivid lights against the dark backdrop was a world away from where she was raised. No color there, just shades of gray and brown.

Ava stepped through the main entrance and paid the fee. The room beyond was an assault on all the senses. Bright, illuminating colors flashed everywhere, the loud music was deafening, and the bass thumped through the floor. A large dance floor dominated the room, filled with hundreds of bodies grinding together to the beat. Ava wished that Jacques had mentioned the usual standards of dress for this place—she was one of few here who wasn't clad in simple neon straps.

Yasmin Hawken

She felt almost overdressed, which considering her previous occupation, was something of a novelty. The building was alive. It felt almost like the barn back home, and the familiarity of the active atmosphere was nice, but how was she going to find Jacques in all these people? She summoned her gauntlet menu and sent him a message.

::Where R U?::

Within seconds of her message being sent, there was a bleep of an incoming notification. It was a map beacon, a way of people coordinating where to meet. She opened the map program, which produced a very basic overview of the club on her AR; on it pulsed an orange marker showing Jacques' location. Feeling a little more confident, she started to press her way through the crowds.

As she made her way through the throngs of people, she could feel the eyes on her. A good whore knew how to carry herself so she showed off all her wares to prospective clients. Years of flaunting herself every time she walked across a room meant she couldn't enter a place without drawing people's gaze. She was pretty, and she knew it. Although, by the beauty standards on this side of the wall, she looked fairly plain. Most people had some form of augment or aesthetic work to enhance their appearance and insisted on wearing as little as possible to show it all off, whereas she was as unaltered as the day she had arrived from The Fringe and far more covered up than most of the other patrons. Not that it stopped the locals from looking at her. Ava wasn't overly interested in any of them. She was done with hooking up with strangers at clubs, and had no intent to start some meaningful relationship with anyone. She was out to look after herself and didn't want to have to deal with someone else's baggage.

She ignored all of the stares she got and, instead, focused on her target, the pulsing orange beacon on the translucent gray map. It took all her concentration to flip between real life and the gauntlet map without walking into something. She didn't care what the public thought, but she didn't want to give them another reason to stare at her. She was having enough trouble being the only dark spot in the otherwise brightly colored crush of humanity around her.

In the back corner of the room, Jacques sat in a booth. She had expected him to be playing on his gauntlet as he had been almost every other time she had seen him, but this time, he sat watching the crowds with a beer clasped between his hands. When he saw her, a small smile tugged at the corners of his mouth. She sighed with relief when she saw that he was dressed in his usual attire. It wasn't that she disliked the way the people around her dressed, but she didn't like sticking out. Not on this side of the wall. She wouldn't let on to him or anyone else that she felt out of place. She strode toward him, allowing nothing in her bearing or expression to show her discomfort.

"Glad to see you found the place alright," he said as he indicated the chair next to him.

"It's much easier when this damn thing works," she said, prodding the band of rubber that was her AR gauntlet.

"Well, it always worked. Don't be mean to the thing because you couldn't use it properly," Jacques teased. "You want a drink?"

"Sure, a beer would be great," she said.

He started to manipulate the AR on the tabletop. It was a simple system that would send a message to the bar, ordering drinks for the table. She watched Jacques' deft motions with rapt concentration; she was envious of the ease of his movements. Technology was such an important thing over here that she was at a severe disadvantage for not being able to use it for the simplest of tasks. His navigations were so fluid and simple, while hers were disjointed and unsure.

"You'll get it," he said. She furrowed her brows; had she spoken aloud?

"Huh?" she said.

"The AR. We'll have you working it with ease in no time. Trust me; I am a fantastic teacher," he said with an air of arrogance. She had to wonder how much of that over-inflated confidence was real and how much was for show.

"Oh, the best. Jacques, you are the true master of all tech," she said flatly, with a roll of her eyes. He looked to her, and even with his goggles obscuring her view, she knew his eyes were focused entirely on her.

"And don't you forget it," he said with a smile.

She shook her head slightly. She was already starting to feel that eye rolling and disbelief were going to become common if she spent more time with Jacques. She sensed that he liked that reaction from people.

Recycled Lives

When the drinks arrived, she found herself clutching the glass tightly and watching as people passed by. Her cautiousness over being spiked was something she hadn't been able to shake even after a conversation with Hamish on the subject. It had happened to her once in The Fringe, and she would never forget that day, nor would she ever let it happen again.

"How is Seattle treating you?" he asked.

"It's nice not to have to shit in a bucket, oh, and of course I love not having crazy gangers chase me," she said with a gulp of her drink.

"Well, at least you had a bucket," he said with a sly grin.

"Oh, don't you start this pissing contest again. You lost last time, and you'll lose again," she said.

The drinks went down smoothly, and the conversation between them flowed nicely. It was mainly insults and sarcastic replies, but that suited her. She didn't like guys who were mushy and overly complimentary. That was just boring and tame. By the time they decided to leave Neon, a light buzz had overtaken her; it had been a while since she had let herself drink enough to truly feel the effects. It showed how much safer she felt here in Seattle.

"Well, I know you ain't gonna have any issues getting back. I'll see you for your next lesson," he said.

There was a brief nod between them before he turned and made his way off down the street. He lived a lot closer than she did. She hailed one of the many automated cabs that stopped outside the club and was quickly on her way back to the Casket. As the city darted by outside the window, she thought over her night.

As much as she had sworn off men, there was something about Jacques that intrigued her, that spoke to a part of her that she thought had long since died. Her upbringing hadn't exactly raised her with a healthy view of relationships; that and watching the train wreck relationships of her fellow Valkyries had killed any want for her to ever find a partner. For the longest time, she had liked the solitude, and now she enjoyed having control over her own body. But something about him had kindled the lonely ember within her. Maybe…just maybe…

Her thought was cut off as the automated system in the cab requested payment. She was glad for the intrusion as her mind was going somewhere that she wasn't wholly comfortable with. There was no way she was actually considering anything. Things were far too messed up. She was far too messed up.

She quickly swiped her chip and paid the charge before slipping out. The mercs either side of the Oaken Casket's door gave her a nod and let her pass without a word. She was starting to enjoy the feeling of living here. The bar was quite busy tonight, and she was glad it was Jackie's shift. The troll-like woman took no shit, and the regulars knew to avoid pissing her off. Right now, Ava felt like she would put someone on their ass if they so much as commented on hers, and spoiled her mood. With a nod to Jackie, Ava slipped under the bar and headed for the backroom she called home. All she wanted right now was sleep.

Recycled Lives

"Morning," said a woman's voice in a Scottish accent. The same accent as Hamish's.

Ava glanced over to a chair in the corner of her room. On it was perched a dainty looking woman with long, straight red hair that fell over her pale, pointed, face. Her left arm was a full chrome augmentic replacement, which was obviously sized to fit her smaller form. Ava had no idea who this woman was or what the hell she was doing in her room. For a moment, all the effects of the alcohol seemed to clear, allowing her complete clarity.

"Can I help you?" Ava asked. She was hyper alert, and currently wishing that she had a ranged weapon of some sort close to hand. The vibe she was getting off this woman was throwing all of her defensive senses into overdrive.

"Yeah, you can, actually. You can stay the hell away from Jacques," she said, and she jumped up from the chair.

"I do what I want, with who I want, thanks. Who the hell do you think you are?" Ava asked, subtly palming the switchblade that she kept on her at all times.

"I thought the accent would give it away. The name's Glass," she said.

Hamish's daughter, Ava thought. Her name was whispered in the bar and never mentioned in front of Hamish. She had no idea what had happened between them, but she had thought it best not to ask any questions.

"I would like to say it's a pleasure, but it's really not," Ava said as she gripped the switchblade tighter. "Now, d'you want to get the hell out of my room?"

The annoyance was quickly turning to anger. She had never been good at taking orders, and now that she had tasted freedom, that was something she wasn't going to relinquish easily. Not to some redhead with what seemed like a power complex. Glass closed the distance between them, the woman ending up only inches from her face.

"Oh, I'm going. But take my warning; stay the fuck away from Jacques. If you don't, you couldn't imagine what will befall you," Glass said before stepping out of the door and closing it behind her.

Ava stood there for a moment just staring at the closed door. Then she snorted derisively and turned away. She wasn't even slightly intimidated by the woman's threats. She had taken down bigger women for stealing her breakfast in The Fringe, and she had access to better weapons now. Besides, how was it Glass' business whatever happened between her and Jacques? He was giving her tech lessons, that was all. With a shake of her head, she locked the door and made for her bed. In the morning, she'd message Jacques and tell him about her unwelcome visitor, but right now, all she wanted was sleep.

*****

The hangover was in full force as Jacques dragged himself to the fridge for a bottle of water. He shouldn't have had so much to drink, but he had enjoyed it so much that he'd lost track of the amount he'd actually had. Since he moved out, he'd been so wrapped up in his feelings for Venom that he hadn't even looked at other women. Ava was different, though. Venom was a lovely girl, pretty, sassy and smart to boot, but she was a good girl in the grand scheme of things. Ava was streetwise, sarcastic, and had a sense of danger about her, like something feral that was only half tame and might swipe at him at any moment, and he found himself really into that.

He grabbed a meal replacement bar and headed back to bed. He was going to spend a few more hours asleep before he would even consider the rest of the day. A bleeping came from his Gauntlet. He looked at the name: Ava. He hadn't expected to hear from her so soon.

"Good evening, how you doing?" he asked, trying to inject a little chirpiness to his voice to try and hide the hangover he was suffering with.

"I'm fine. Just wanted to know why I am being threatened to stay away from you," Ava said in an annoyed tone.

"What? Who the hell is threatening you?" Jacques asked. Why the hell would anyone have a problem with them hanging out?

"A lovely woman called Glass," she said sarcastically. "When I got home from the club this morning, she was in my room waiting for me."

Glass! God, it had been a long time since he'd even heard the name. Just the mention of her got his adrenaline pumping. The emotions he felt were very mixed. He was relieved that she was okay, but at the same time, he felt guilty as hell. Glass was his ex-girlfriend and teenhood sweetheart; even seeing Ava in a platonic way had made him feel like he was cheating on her. Adding his unrequited feelings for Venom into the mix was like adding hot sauce to a dish that was already going to give him indigestion. He knew it wasn't a completely rational feeling, given that he wasn't currently in a relationship with any of them, but the churning in his gut didn't ease any with the knowledge.

"Oh," he said simply.

"Someone you know then?" Ava asked, her tone implying she wasn't overly happy. "Want to fill me in?"

"Yeah…umm…sure. She's my ex; we broke up a long time ago," Jacques explained. A pit of nausea was quickly forming in his stomach as he thought back to that situation.

"So jealous ex? Any more to this story?" she asked.

Jacques sighed. He wanted to tell her everything, but a phone call seemed impersonal.

"Can we meet later tonight? Then I'll tell you everything," he said. Silence fell on the other end of the call. The time spent waiting felt like years as he worried he was going to get completely rejected.

"Okay," she said.

They made quick plans of a time and place before ending the call. He wasn't sure why he cared so much about what Ava thought, but he did. Before he met her, he had something that he needed to do. Calling up

Recycled Lives

Hamish's number, he hit dial; as soon as the call was answered, he spoke.

"Where is she, Hamish?" he asked.

"Puyallup, 1478 114th," Hamish replied without a beat. Jacques liked that Hamish didn't even have to ask who he was talking about.

"Thanks," Jacques said and hung up the phone.

The effects of the hangover had been completely destroyed by the sudden influx of information. The fact that Glass was back in the picture had hit him hard. He had no idea that she was in the city, and was quite angry that Hamish hadn't told him. His feelings for Glass were a complicated ball of love, dislike, jealousy, concern, and so much more that he couldn't even pin them down. The one thing he knew for sure was that he had to see her.

He dressed and grabbed his pack before heading out of the building. Usually, he skated everywhere, but today, he felt the need for haste. He grabbed the first Silver Bullet bus that drove past and made his way to Puyallup. During the trip, his mind regurgitated everything that had ever happened between them. The good, the bad…just everything. She was his first love and great loss, and that was something he would never forget.

When everything had gone wrong, he had pined for her. Sitting in his jail cell, he'd sent her message after message, but hadn't had a single response. With everything that had happened, it was her that he had wanted to talk to. He had needed to talk to her, he had needed her forgiveness most of all, but it had never happened. When he'd gotten out of jail, he'd hoped to talk to her and make things right, but she had been nowhere to be found. He'd heard whispers from the staff at the Oaken Casket, and none of it was good.

Glass had never been sweet and innocent. She swore like a sailor and loved nothing more than a barroom brawl, but she had always had good intentions and a kind heart. From what he had heard, she had been following the wrong path ever since the incident.

When he reached the house, he stood on the curb, just looking at the two story house. It looked so normal. He hoped that he'd ring that bell, and he'd find her exactly the way she used to be. Just good old Glass, but knowing that she'd threatened Ava, he didn't think that was likely. With a deep breath, he approached the door and knocked. The anxiety was weighing on him as both sides of him warred as to whether he wanted Glass to be here or not.

When the door opened, he was taken aback by the woman before him. The features looked like Glass, but they were somehow sharper and harsher than he remembered. Her trademark long red hair no longer fell to near her waist and no longer hid half her face. Her clothing style had changed, too. The tops were more daringly cut, exposing more of her tattoo covered skin. The imposing black marks were also new. With the addition of the full chromed augmented arm, she looked worlds away from the sweet brawler he once knew.

"Well, well, well. I wondered when I'd see you," she said almost seductively as she leaned on the doorframe.

Recycled Lives

"You know I have this thing called a gauntlet. You could have just messaged me rather than threatening my friend," Jacques said, trying to seem nonchalant.

"If I'd called, would you have come?" she asked.

He didn't have an immediate response for that question. He had questioned his feelings for her a lot over the years. He had actually thought he was over her, but seeing her standing there had just reignited the spark that he'd thought was long since extinguished. But with it came the bitter reminder of what she had done to him. That she had ignored him all these years, and had never checked in on him when he was inside. When he had needed her more than anyone else in the world, she hadn't been there. It was only now that his life was getting back together that she had come out of the woodwork looking for him.

"Glass, I don't know what kind of game you're playing, but leave Ava out of it, okay?" Jacques said sharply, trying to stay clear of the subject of their shared history.

"Do you want to come in? Have a drink?" Glass asked, indicating inside as if she hadn't heard him at all.

Something about her entire demeanor was off. He didn't know whether the conversation was intentionally disjointed or if it was a ploy to throw him off, but something wasn't right. There were the remnants of some red powder under her nose, her eyes were slightly bloodshot, and there was a slight jitter to her hand. She was flying high on something.

Yasmin Hawken

A part of him called to go inside and look after her like he would have done for the old Glass, but he knew that it wasn't the right move to make. If he followed her in, they would end up in bed together, and he would enjoy the time with her and would want to forget all those transgressions and shared pain. Then he would hate himself, and he would feel even more horrendous than he did already. His emotions were such a mess right now that he didn't want to risk getting himself into any situations with her.

"Just stay away from Ava, alright," Jacques said. He turned and headed straight back to the curb before he betrayed himself.

Rather than waiting for the bus, he started down the street at a brisk walk. He needed away from her and away from that house. He would catch the bus a few stops down when he was far enough away that he didn't have to worry about running back to her.

Chapter Six

As darkness started to fall, Lucinda woke up in her boyfriend's arms. She smiled as she snuggled into his smooth, muscled chest. This was definitely something that she could do every day. She looked up at Zane. He was still fast asleep, his face calm and relaxed—something rarely seen by anybody. She ran a finger gently over his chin, and his rough stubble scratched gently. She ran her finger over his lips and jumped when he gently nipped her finger.

"Holy shit," she swore as her heart started hammering in her chest.

"Evening," he said cheekily.

He laughed as he wrapped his arms tighter and pulled her against him. His smile lit up his entire face as he reached up and pushed her hair out of her face before placing a gentle kiss against her lips.

"You scared the shit out of me," she said. She was still trying to convince her heart that she wasn't under attack after the early morning surprise.

"I couldn't help myself," he said with a smile.

Yasmin Hawken

He kissed the top of her forehead before slipping out from beneath the sheets. She lay back on the bed and watched his naked back, her eyes tracing the lines of muscles before she reached his round and firm butt. He was a beautiful specimen of a man, and he was all hers. He stopped in the mirror and scratched at his stubble, his other hand tapping the chrome full augmented leg he had. She had a feeling he was a lot more self-conscious about the replacement than he would ever admit to anyone.

"You're going to have to put clothes on, or else I'm never going to get up," Lucinda said as she tore her eyes from him and rolled onto her back.

"Are you working today?" he asked as he grabbed a towel from the linen cupboard.

"I've got some training later on this morning, but I was going to spend this evening lazing around the house," she explained. If she was going to move in here, she was going to have to get used to being here without him.

"Well, I could pick you up after training and bring you back if you like," he said.

"Sure thing," she said with a huge smile. She loved riding the bike almost as much as she loved riding the biker.

He leaned in and kissed her before he stepped into the bathroom. She listened to the water start to run before she finally got up the courage to drag herself of bed and get dressed. She was feeling nice and calm as she headed downstairs to the kitchen, deciding what to cook for breakfast.

Recycled Lives

As she stepped into the kitchen, she saw Sawyer sitting at the table. Open in front of her was Lucinda's makeup bag, its contents spread across the kitchen table. Using the small mirror from the pack, she was painting her face with Lucinda's makeup. Lucinda didn't know exactly what to do or say.

"Hey, Sawyer," Lucinda said awkwardly.

"Hey," Sawyer said without looking up.

"You seem to be using my makeup," Lucinda said.

"Mine ran out," Sawyer said. The girl didn't speak much. She spent most of her time hidden in her room, or quietly hovering in the background while the rest of the family bickered.

"Did you not think to ask?" Lucinda asked, feeling slightly frustrated.

"No," Sawyer said.

"You know you should really ask before you use other people's things," Lucinda said.

"Oh. Okay," was Sawyer's only response.

There was no emotion in the girl's voice, no apology, no nothing. Lucinda wasn't quite sure what else to do. She didn't mind Sawyer using her makeup, but the fact that she hadn't asked irritated her. There didn't seem to be any line when it came to people's belongings or personal space. She had at least expected an apology or an acknowledgment of wrongdoing, but, no, there was nothing. Sawyer just carried on doing her makeup.

Lucinda left her to it and went to the stove. She was lost in her own thoughts as she started to grab the things she needed to make pancakes. Should she explain to Sawyer why she was in the wrong or should she just leave it? She wasn't sure Sawyer would understand, and even if she did, Lucinda doubted she would listen. She should just leave it. She tried to push the thought to the back of her mind as she started preparing breakfast for the family—a colossal undertaking in its own right.

From behind, she heard the makeup bag snap closed. She glanced around to see Sawyer getting up from the table.

"You gonna have your breakfast first?" Lucinda said.

Sawyer stopped and looked to her. It was like she was eyeing up the danger of the situation. Sawyer was a tall, well-toned, beautiful girl, with long blonde hair, an angular face, and the same dark eyes as Zane. She also shared Zane's take no shit attitude. Even after leaving The Fringe, all the kids still focused on their self-defense. Lucinda didn't think that was something that they would ever stop honing.

Sawyer walked over to grab a plate. She was a little taller and more muscular than Lucinda, and sometimes she could be a little intimidating. It didn't help that out of all the family, she was the hardest to talk to. Caspian was arrogant and aggressive to Zane, but to her, he'd been nothing but a sweetheart. Sawyer just creeped her out a little. She was too quiet and watchful. It often felt like she was sitting in the corner planning something.

Sawyer took a plate and grabbed the condiments for the pancakes. She turned to walk away but quickly turned back.

"Thank you," she said before heading back to the table and laying the condiments out for everyone else to use. Lucinda smiled a little to herself; please and thank you were definitely an improvement.

Moments later, there was an influx of family. The noise and excitement as she handed out the plates of pancakes rebounded off the walls, making it sound like there was twice the number of children in the room. The table was quickly filled by the kids as they scarfed down their food. It always reminded her of the orphanages. So much chatter and energy. She guessed it was one of the reasons she liked being here. It felt like home. It was a shame that her recent interaction with Sawyer hung over her like a cloud. It was difficult getting along with her when she only came over every few days. How difficult would it be if she lived here full time?

Zane came into the kitchen and walked over to her. Wrapping an arm around her waist he pulled her into another kiss, an action that never failed to leave her a little breathless. She gave him a slight smile before handing him a plate.

"You okay?" he asked.

"Huh, yeah, why?" she asked.

"You have a face on that says something's bothering you," he replied. Since they'd started dating, he'd become really good at reading her emotions.

"I had an issue with Sawyer this morning. That's all," Lucinda explained quietly. "Don't worry about it."

"No, tell me," he insisted. "Come on, Luce, what's going on?"

"I came in to find her using my makeup. She didn't ask, and she gave no apology or recognition that she shouldn't have taken it. Nothing. Just felt a little like she didn't respect me or my stuff, that's all," Lucinda explained.

"Shit. I should have told you this before, but I thought we'd got through this." Zane sighed as he dragged his hand through his hair, then he lowered his voice. "Sawyer had a really big issue with 'sticky fingers'. She got in a lot of trouble when we first arrived here."

"What happened?" Lucinda asked.

Zane leaned back against the sideboard. With a sigh, he dragged his hand down over his face and glanced back to the table. The look in his eyes said he was reliving something that he would rather not. She touched his arm gently, and he looked at her with a smile that didn't reach his eyes.

"Back in The Fringe, I had trouble providing the kids with what they needed, especially in the first few years after Mom and Dad died. Too many kids, and they were too young to earn their own keep. If we got low on funds or food, I would cut back eating. When Sawyer found out, she started stealing from the market to make sure there was enough food for me, too," Zane said; he obviously blamed himself for her having to do that. "When we got to Seattle, she had been doing it for so long that she couldn't stop. She stole whatever she wanted from shops, from school, or even people on the street."

"Ah," Lucinda said. She wanted to say something but couldn't conjure any words to fit.

Recycled Lives

"Yeah. So after many talks with the school, the police, and the Network having to cover my ass a couple of times, we finally seemed have it under control," Zane explained. The stress was evident on his face. "I'll have a word with her. Let her know it's not okay at home, either."

He headed to the table, indicating to Sawyer and then the living room, with a stern look on his face. She could have had the conversation with Sawyer herself, but sometimes the kids' reactions weren't in line with what you would expect. She'd seen Caspian throw a punch at Zane because he'd eaten the last donut for Christ's sake.

Lucinda was feeling pretty shit about stressing him out, but was also feeling concerned about her future here. If Sawyer had a habit of taking things, she wasn't sure she wanted to bring her belongings here. She had a lot of paint and canvases that were expensive to replace, and several items with sentimental value that she had left from before her parents disappeared. This morning, she had felt so good about moving in, but now she was starting to question if it was actually a good idea at all.

Chapter Seven

After seeing Glass, Jacques had been a mess. His natural instinct had been to find the first bar and drink until he couldn't feel the pain anymore, but he was meeting Ava later on this evening, and turning up wasted was bad form. Instead, he'd spent his evening walking the streets of Seattle Central; it was something he did when he felt lost or disconnected. He'd even checked in with some of his contacts in the homeless network. The guys always had something that needed doing, and several simply like to talk the ear off anyone who would listen. Anything to try and distract him from his thoughts. Little helped.

Before he knew it, the time was coming up for him to meet Ava. The closer he came to meeting her, the sicker he felt. He was so nervous having to recite his history with Glass to someone else. He hadn't even told Lucy about his past. At first, he nearly had himself convinced that the nerves came from the shame of what happened between them and the life that had been lost. The truth was he was quickly coming to like

Ava. Her hard woman, give-no-shit attitude had really rubbed off on him, and he was actually nervous that his story would cause her to leave or to not like him anymore. It made him feel stupid. The only person he'd really cared that much about had been Glass. It was ironic that a conversation about his ex could be the one to stop anything happening with someone new. That's if she was even interested in him.

There was a jingle as he pushed the door to the diner open. It was a quiet greasy spoon, making it the perfect place to talk about dark histories and evil exes, but probably the worst place for a first date. Not that it was a date, no. It was just him telling his story.

He spotted Ava immediately. She was sequestered away into a corner booth, staring into a cup of coffee that she was stirring continuously with her spoon. For the first time, her hair was tied back, and just that simple change made her face seem harder and more serious. He took a deep breath before crossing the room and settling into the booth opposite her. She looked up to him without a trace of emotion on her harsh features.

"You alright?" Jacques asked with a smile. She didn't reply in kind. Instead, she leaned back in the booth, crossing her arms.

"Well, just watching my back, y'know. I might get shanked just for meeting you here," she said sarcastically. "Let's get straight to the point, shall we?"

"Yeah, let's," he said and paused as he tried to work out exactly what to say. Trying to sum up his history in a few concise sentences was hard. He felt exactly like he did at his court hearing, but for some reason, the outcome of this meeting felt so much more important. "Glass…she's my ex-girlfriend…"

"You got a great choice in women," she said with a slight smirk. Jacques gave a strained smile at the comment; it didn't last long as he thought about the next part of the story.

"She wasn't always like this," Jacques said with a sad sigh. "She's always had a wild streak, but this dark edge she's taken on was all my fault."

"What happened?" she asked. The hardness was starting to disappear from her voice, and she seemed a little more interested.

"It was a few years back now. Glass had a stalker for about six months. The guy would sit in the bar for hours, bump into her on the street, interact with all her social media posts, stuff like that. She was pretty freaked out, but he'd never done anything for the cops to get involved. I'd been out looking for work one day. I came home to find him cuddled up next to her in our bed. To be honest, I thought she had cheated on me. Then he woke up and saw me, yelled something, then threw himself at me. I panicked and grabbed the bedside lamp and hit him with it. I hit him a little too hard and well… He died," Jacques said. He stared past her at the grubby wall of the diner. He would remember that night for the rest of his life. There was a part of him that was forever darkened by that moment, and nothing he could ever do would fix it.

A spark shot through him the moment Ava's hand rested on his. He looked at her and gave her a slight smile. There was more to the story, and he needed to finish it before he lost all strength.

"Glass was woken up by the yelling. She was so confused and lying next to a dead man. It turned out he was an old ex-boyfriend who was still sore that she ditched him for being overly grabby and possessive of her. Wouldn't let her go out of the house on her own, and woe betide her if she talked to, or even so much as glanced at another guy. That sort of stuff. She told me he was completely obsessed with the idea of trying to get her back. She always had a terrible taste in guys. I wasn't any better," Jacques said sadly.

"You aren't a bad guy for protecting someone you love," Ava said.

"Nice of you to say it like that. I don't think Glass would agree. Last thing she said to me was that I was just as bad as him. She knew I had thought, even for just a second, that she would get her kicks with another man, in our bed. That she was a no-good slut who would open her legs for anyone who asked. I couldn't really dispute that—for a few seconds that's exactly what I thought. I went to prison for a year, and in that time, she never wrote a letter or bothered to call. Nothing when I got out, either," he explained.

He wished he'd ordered a drink just for an excuse to sip at something so he didn't feel the need to fill the tense silence. All he could focus on was the feeling of her soft fingers on the back of his hand. Making a ballsy move, he moved his hand so he could hold hers. He stroked her long fingers, watching her subtly for her reaction. It was very slight, but her shoulders sagged a little in relaxation.

"So that's it. That's the basic saga of Glass and me. I don't know why she is threatening you to stay away, 'cos she hasn't bothered with me for years. Maybe the idea of someone else has sparked her interest again. Now you know the story, you can choose whether you want to stay or leave," he said.

With the offer put before her on the table, his stomach was doing somersaults. She didn't really move at all; she sat there looking at him as if trying to figure out what to do. The longer the seconds stretched, the sicker he was feeling. God, she needed to make a decision. His heart thudding in his chest couldn't take any more.

*****

Ava had been really mad when she had come to the diner. She thought she had left random break-ins and threats back in The Fringe. This was why she didn't get attached to people, and the fact that she thought she had found something good only to have it start to turn sour had left her on edge. When she had sat waiting for him to get started, she had even considered getting up and leaving, but as soon as he had begun to tell his story, she could see the emotion, all of that regret.

When he put that decision on the table, she already knew what she would do, but there was a part of her that enjoyed the moment of worry on his face. The fact was it was the first time in a very long time someone actually cared about any decision that she had to make. It was nice to feel cared about. Like her opinions or wishes actually mattered. The way his fingers caressed her hand was so delicate, no demanding touch or aggressive intention. It was totally unlike any experience she had ever had with any of the johns in The Fringe—all grabbing hands, possession, and eagerness to take their chosen currency's worth. She forced down the unpleasant memories of that time and place, focusing instead on Jacques' nervous caress.

"Well, I think you need to buy me another coffee and possibly a stack of pancakes and bacon," she said cheekily. "Then maybe we can talk some more."

His eyebrows shot up in surprise. It seemed he in no way expected a positive response. She gave him a small smile before she drained the rest of the coffee and pushed the cup to the edge of the table.

"You think one threat is enough to get me to stop? The Fringe breeds you tougher than that," she said with a chuckle.

Her annoyance had been genuine, but that didn't mean she was scared. When she had lay down to sleep after her visit from Glass, she had found herself getting more and more annoyed. If she had been in the Fringe, she would have hit the woman for just having the audacity to come into her room. She probably could get away with it in the Oaken Casket, but she had to moderate her behavior for the rest of Seattle. The fake chip in her hand was good enough to use day to day, but too much scrutiny, and its authenticity could be questioned. As a result, she needed to stay clear of the security. She wanted this fresh start, and she didn't want to be arrested for being chipless.

"I went and saw Glass earlier today. I told her to leave you alone. I doubt she'll listen, mind; that girl is a law unto herself," Jacques explained.

Recycled Lives

She could see the concern on his face. There was something about that, that warmed her heart. It was a feeling she hadn't experienced in a very long time. When you sold sex for your survival, people acted like they cared because that's what they felt like they should. You could always tell when they meant it and when it was false. Jacques wasn't lying. He did actually care what she thought, and that had to be why he came and told his story.

"Honestly, if she shows up again, then I'll show her what girls from The Fringe are really like," she said with a slightly sadistic grin. It had been a while since she had a good tussle and would welcome the excuse.

"Just play it safe, alright? Don't want you getting yourself in shit because of me," Jacques said.

"Alright, alright. Enough of this sharing is caring shit. It's getting a little sappy up in here," she said with a smile. The feelings of care and concern were getting a little too real for her. She couldn't let someone close; they always just let her down or got her hurt. "So let's talk about something, anything other than your crazy assed ex."

"How are things over at the Oaken Casket?" Jacques asked.

"Is that the only question you're ever gunna ask me?" she said with a smirk. The job may seem simple to most but it was going to be the key to getting everything she wanted. She glanced out the window. Fat droplets of rain were splattering against the glass and snaking their way down. "It's good. A lot of work, but I enjoy the people. Apart from the handsy mercs, but Hamish sees to that pretty fast."

"Hey, it's a good starting point. Hamish is good like that, doesn't let any harm come to his staff or his well-behaved regulars," Jacques responded.

"He is. He gave me hassle last week because I worked a shift without eating," she said with a chuckle, remembering the look on the man's face. He was the deadbeat Rider Father she never had. "Talking about food, I'm pretty sure you owe me pancakes and bacon."

Suddenly, they were interrupted by an almighty crack of thunder and a bright flash of lightning. Somewhere in the cafe, someone yelped loudly at the noise before breaking into giggles at their reaction. Ava looked out the window, staring up the street at the sky between the huge monoliths of glass and steel, hoping to catch another flash of lightning.

"How about we get those to go? I wanna take you somewhere," Jacques said with excitement on his face.

"Sure," she replied.

Jacques made a quick order, paying more to get the food quicker. With the food and drinks in hand, they stepped outside, and Jacques grabbed her hand. Instinctively, she went to pull away, but at the last second stopped herself. He led her through the streets. Crowds of people had their collars turned up, and their umbrellas opened against the rain. She and Jacques didn't have any wet weather gear except the coats on their backs. Ava wanted to know where they were going, but there was something about the look on his face that had her excited in spite of her instinctive distrust of the unknown. In The Fringe, surprises were usually unpleasant and deadly, but her instinct told her that Jacques wouldn't let her come to harm.

They came to stop beneath a large apartment block. With the gold buzzer plate on the side, it seemed like a pretty upscale place. Why the hell were they at apartments? It wasn't even his place. She was a little confused.

"What are we doing?" she asked as Jacques ascended the steps.

"Just trust me; it'll be good," he said confidently as he strode up to the door.

She watched as he pulled something card-like from his pocket and stuck it in the slot beside the door. He held his chip over the scanner, and the door clicked open. He took her hand and led her inside. The inside really was lavish; a plush deep blue carpet ran down the center of the room, and the walls were the perfect balance of gold and cream. It was clean and tidy and didn't smell like piss, unlike a lot of the lower class areas of the city.

"How the hell do you have access to a place like this?" she asked, looking around a little awestruck.

"A couple years back, I broke in here to lift a few things. I managed to get myself put on the system as a resident. If I was really hard up for somewhere to stay, I'd camp down in the basement for the night," he explained as he made his way to the block of elevators.

"So why are we here now?" she asked.

"Be patient," he said.

They stepped inside the elevator, and Jacques hit the button for the top floor. Her anticipation mounted. Was he taking her to meet someone? She wanted to ask a ton of questions, but the sly smirk that was ever present on his face indicated he wasn't going to say anything.

The elevator came to a stop, and they stepped out onto another elegant-looking floor that could only be one of the penthouses she had read about in the gossip articles Jackie like to show her. There were only five doors on the entire floor, which meant that the apartments up here must be a damn sight bigger than the back room that she was renting out. She wondered why people would need this much space? What was the point in furniture, artwork, and all that jazz? It was just stuff to get stolen, broken, or in your way when trying to make a quick exit. All you needed was food and water to live. Unless it was required to survive, she didn't understand the point of materialistic things.

"You coming?" Jacques asked, dragging her from her thoughts.

He was standing to the side of the elevator, his hand resting on the wall. It took her a moment to notice the small door that was painted to look like the wall. With trepidation in her mind, she made her way towards him. They headed inside. It was a maintenance cupboard decorated in bottles of chemicals, mops, brooms and wet floor signs. They passed through a second door and followed a set of stairs upwards until they reached a third door with a sign that read 'Roof Access'.

As she stepped out onto the roof, the cool wind encircled her, bringing with it the light showering of rain. She was immediately distracted by the sight before her. All around her were the lights of Seattle.

Recycled Lives

Neon signs illuminating the dark city, people's apartment lights flickering on and off, and on the street far below, the lights of the cars sped by. Her jaw nearly hit the floor at the breathtaking sight of the city before her. She had never been up this high in her life. The forty-story elegant apartment block acted as the venue for the most beautiful show she had ever seen. She took a few steps away from Jacques, mesmerized.

"Watch out!" Jacques said, grabbing her hand and pulling her back.

Her heart was instantly hammering at his alarm as she jumped back beside him. She quickly looked around to see what had caused his concern. All she saw was a metal pole sticking out of the ground before her.

"Trust me when I say you don't want to stand near that," Jacques said. He led her around the edge of the roof and perched on the thick barrier that surrounded the edge of the roof. The ornate decoration made for a perfect seat. He tapped beside him.

"So are you going to tell me why we're here?" she asked.

"Just sit down," he said with a smirk.

As she took the seat beside him, he removed his goggles and put them away in his pack. Ava had never seen him take his goggles off. His face seemed different, longer, with high cheekbones that she hadn't seen before. He took the two packs of food from the cafe out of his backpack and handed her one. The scent of him opening his food container was enough to cause her stomach to rumble. She was just about to open hers when there was an almighty crack of lightning. Ava jumped, her heart hammering in her chest. The bolt had struck the roof merely feet in front of her.

"You're safe, don't worry," Jacques said with a slight chuckle. "That spike in the ground is a lightning rod; it draws the electricity from the sky to protect the building. Just sit and watch."

She fell silent for a moment as she watched the spike with bated breath waiting and hoping for another lightning strike. She wasn't disappointed. There was a rumble in the sky followed by an almighty crack. A streak of blue lightning hit the roof again, the flash illuminating the roof brightly for all of a matter of seconds. The bright blue lightning strike disappeared as fast as it arrived.

"That's beautiful," Ava said in complete awe.

*****

The lightning was beautiful, but it was nothing in comparison to the woman before him. With each strike, her eyes lit up with childlike glee. Each strike illuminated her face, lighting her up with complete awe. He wanted to reach out and take her hand, maybe even kiss her, but he doubted that would be well received. That wasn't the Ava that he had been getting to know.

"How does it work?" Ava asked abruptly. He was quickly drawn from the fantasy of kissing her and forced his brain to be logical.

Recycled Lives

"Umm... Well, the metal is more conductive than anything nearby, so it attracts and allows the electricity a safe passage to the ground. So when the lightning strikes, it protects the building from taking damage," he explained. He often forgot that her education wasn't great, and he really didn't want her to feel stupid, so he didn't overcomplicate it.

"It's amazing," she said. Her hands gripped the edge of the roof as she watched intently.

The beauty of this building was its height. If there was a lightning storm, this building was quite often hit, as he had learned after months of squatting here. Many a night he had spent up here watching nature at its finest. This was the first time he'd ever brought someone here to share it with him. He was glad it was her.

"Don't forget the food that you extorted out of me," he joked as he forced himself to focus on something other than the perfect curve of her jaw.

"Oh, yeah," she said as she flicked open the container and started on her own food.

Another strike of lightning brought a strange effect to Jacques's eyes. The black market augmentic enhancements weren't properly insulated—a risk you took with black market equipment. Whenever he was too close to live electric, they had a particularly interesting effect. The whole world's colors would become flipped or distorted. Right now, the world was dancing in pastel hues, and the whole image waved gently. It was almost hallucinogenic.

Yasmin Hawken

"I wish you could see the world as I do right now," he said, the rose gold colors making the whole scene somewhat romantic.

"How is it different?" she asked, looking to him with intrigue.

"Well, the world dances with colors that it shouldn't. My eyewear will need recalibration later, but the effect is beautiful. It makes things seem a little magical and so unreal," he said honestly as he looked to her. "You look beautiful."

She smiled. God, that smile was so bright, and so unfitting with the hardened demeanor she had shown all this time. No stoic looks, no tight-lipped smiles, just a full beaming smile. He hadn't thought she could look any more beautiful, but somehow, she just kept surprising him.

Before he stopped himself, he reached out and cupped her chin, his thumb running over a small scar on her jawline. He was trying to work up the courage to kiss her, but a part of him was worried she'd actually throw him off the roof. Before he could make his move, she did. Leaning in, she pressed her lips against his.

The kiss was intense, no delicate movements, just passion and wanting. Everything that he imagined a first kiss should be. His hand tangled in her long hair as he deepened the kiss. He didn't want it to end. When they broke apart, both of them were slightly out of breath. He rested his forehead against hers for a moment before she turned and looked out over the city. The lights reflected in her eyes.

"Thank you," she said.

"What for?" he asked, his eyebrows creasing in confusion.

"For making me feel like a person. For making me feel like I matter," she said without looking at him. Her gaze stared firmly at the large dark blob on the horizon. The Fringe.

"You *do* matter, and I'll keep showing you that. And keep you safe," Jacques said. "I promise."

When her fingers wrapped around his, the world felt complete as he felt something click into place inside him. Nothing could ever feel better than this moment.

Chapter Eight

Ava was wiping down the bar; it had been another busy shift, and she was looking forward to getting some sleep. There had been two fights break out in the bar today, and both involved new, baby-faced mercs who were trying to throw their weight around. The fights were ended quickly by the veterans; it would be a long old while until those kids came back. If they were lucky, they might have had time to grow some facial hair by then.

She tossed the cloth in the sink and turned to find India staring at her. India was the daughter of one of the big named mercs, a close friend of Hamish's. When he went away on business, the sixteen-year-old stayed here under the watchful eye of the merc band. Ava had met her a few times; the girl always looked at her with intrigue.

"Ava, can I ask you a favor?" India asked.

"What's that?" Ava asked, already concerned about what the request could be.

"Well, this weekend I'm going to this party, and the guy I like is going to be there. I really need to make sure he notices me. You always look so good, like you're so off trend that it's basically a new trend. I need someone to look over my outfits and help me decide. So will you help me? Please?" India asked.

Ava stood there a little awkwardly, unsure what to make of the request. She was a little flattered that India had thought to come to her, and that she was 'off trend', whatever that meant. Fashion had never really been a thing in The Fringe. The only people who really cared about what they wore were the gangers. A person in the wrong colors on your turf was a threat to be dealt with, even if it just turned out they were an innocent bystander later on. It was the price of the shoot first, ask questions later mentality that all the gangs had. Ava dragged her mind from the depths of The Fringe and forced herself to focus on the girl in front of her.

"Sure, I'll do what I can," Ava said with a shrug.

India basically bounced along the corridor back to her room. Ava followed slowly behind her. She had had plans to research Seattle's laws on murder in self-defense in case Glass decided to come around again. Then she was going to sleep and hopefully dream of killing that interfering bitch. But she could spare some time to look at some clothes; it would make the younger girl happy.

India's room was sparse, with a standard bed, wardrobe, side table, and sink that all of the Casket back rooms had. India had immediately thrown open a travel case that sat on the end of the bed and was pulling items out of it while chattering on about some AR personality that Ava had never heard of. Ava leaned against the walls, arms crossed over her chest, foot propped up as she waited for the 'fashion show' to begin.

India tried on three different outfits that clearly hadn't been made for someone of her age, or with her body type in mind. The material either stretched out in the wrong places or hung off her giving her the impression of someone wearing their older siblings' clothing. The colors weren't flattering, either. The military greens and khaki gave a sickly hue to her skin.

"So which one do you think is the best?" India asked.

There was the darker side of Ava that considered just telling her the best of the shit so she could go to bed, but there was a part of her that couldn't do that. If she was going to survive in Seattle, she had to fight against everything she had been before. The girl had asked for help, and she was going to do her best.

"Honestly, none of them look good on you. They don't sit right, and you looked plain uncomfortable. Wear something you like, and if he doesn't like it, fuck him," Ava said. She was tainted when it came to the idea of relationships, but this side of the wall they seemed to chase them. The best thing this girl could do was be herself; no point changing for anyone.

A look of sadness crossed India's face, and she looked crestfallen. There was a swirl of guilt in Ava's stomach. She had been a little harsh. She needed to remind herself of how old she was. In The Fringe, she would been seen as an adult, but over here, she was still seen as a kid and therefore treated like one.

"Y'know, if you really want this then I might be able to tailor some of this stuff to look or fit better," Ava said as she stalked over to the bed and started to look through the clothes she had.

"You can?" India said, her eyes lighting up.

"Yeah, just let me look," Ava said.

Once she had looked through the pile of clothes, she headed back to her room and fetched her sewing kit. One well-used sewing kit that had been used on skin as well as clothes. How her life had changed. She got India to try on one of the tops and pairs of pants and made her stand still while she added stitches to mark where to make changes. It was simple and wouldn't take her long. It only really needed to last a night anyway.

"Where do you buy your clothes?" India asked.

"I mainly buy cheap and alter the stuff I want. No point wasting money on something that you can make," Ava said absentmindedly.

"Man, that's so cool. You know, with your style, you could make so much money. So many people are into the 'off trend' trend," India said.

As Ava quickly made the stitches in the clothes, she thought about what India had said. Maybe she was actually good at something other than fucking and fighting. Maybe there was a skill that she could bring to Seattle. She could take the grungy, Fringe style clothes and sell them to people as a completely new style of fashion. It wasn't hard; she'd been looking at Fringe clothes her entire life.

"There, done," Ava said as she handed the clothes over. The alterations were minor, but they were exactly what she had wanted. She had to trash one of the tops, but it made the other look so much better.

"Oh my god, that's amazing," India said, spinning around in circles.

"You should borrow this," Ava said as she shrugged off her leather jacket and handed it over. "It will be a good finish. I want it back, though."

The girl gushed thanks at her and squealed a lot more than Ava was comfortable with. It almost took her needing a crowbar to leave the room. She felt some thankfulness for India, though. She had showed her that she wasn't completely useless in this world. She had something to bring to it. She made her way back to her room with the plan to start searching the Nexus for Seattle fashion. See if she really could do something. Her future suddenly felt a whole lot brighter.

Chapter Nine

It had been a few days since Jacques' evening with Ava. He hadn't stopped thinking about it since, the setting, the kiss. Everything had suited them to a tee—no traditional fancy restaurant dinner and a pricey theatre show for them. They had sent a few messages back and forth since, but he wanted to take her out again. He'd been trying to find an excuse for them to meet up, but in the end, he had just settled for heading down to the Casket for a drink. It wouldn't be too big of a deal; he drank there all the time, since before he joined the Network. He had been there a lot less of late, but his presence wasn't so infrequent that anyone would think anything of him being there.

As he walked down the steps in the basement bar, the usual sights greeted him. This place hadn't changed in years, and he didn't expect it would. The regulars and the ownership liked it just as it was. He took a seat at the bar.

"If you are looking for Ava, you might as well head back out; she ain't here," Hamish said with a chuckle as he stopped before him.

"I have no idea what you are talking about. Are you gonna get me a beer or not?" Jacques asked with an awkward laugh.

"Sure you don't. You have no idea about the date you had with my bartender the other night," Hamish said with knowing smirk.

Jacques had no idea how to reply to that. Hamish had nearly been his father-in-law at one point. He had been so in love with Glass that he'd actually been considering proposing to her. Even after everything that had gone wrong between them, he really didn't like the idea of telling her Father that he liked someone else. Hamish had been there for him when nobody else was.

"Did she tell you?" Jacques asked.

"No, I'm just a fucking mind reader," Hamish said sarcastically as he slid a bottle of beer over the bar to Jacques.

"You know, old man, one day that sass is going to be the end of you," Jacques said cockily.

"It'll take a lot to kill me, Jacques, don't you worry," Hamish responded. "So are you going to tell me about this date?"

"It wasn't a date, not really," Jacques said. Food, a kiss, lightning, who was he kidding? It was a fucking date; he just wasn't willing to admit it.

"You going to tell me about it?" Hamish asked. Jacques was really wishing that he would drop this line of questioning. It was a really awkward conversation to have with your ex's Father.

Recycled Lives

"What are we, gossiping girls? Wanna braid my hair while we talk?" Jacques replied sarcastically, giving Hamish a smile.

The old man laughed and shook his head before making his way to the other end of the bar to serve another customer. Jacques wasn't exactly sure what to do with his time now. He had hoped to chat with Ava until the end of her shift and then maybe get something to eat. Maybe he should just hang around here and have some time with the regulars, because he needed to spend some time keeping his connections up. There was no way he was just staying so that he had a chance of seeing Ava when she got back. Nope. No way.

"I think she will be good for you," Hamish said. Jacques jumped a little. He hadn't realized the man had even come back from serving.

"Why do you say that?" Jacques asked.

"She's just broken enough for you," Hamish said. Jacques' brows creased in confusion.

"I'm not sure if that is a compliment or an insult," Jacques said with a slight smile.

"A compliment. With your past, you need someone who can understand the shit you've been through, and who isn't going to judge you for it," Hamish explained.

Jacques had never considered that. Glass may have had a hard demeanor, but she was by no means broken when they dated. The worst that ever came to her were guys that got too handsy in the bar, and she would usually end that with a hard hit from the closest bottle or glass. Whereas Ava had some hard times in her past, something he could very much empathize with.

"Well, you've got a point there," Jacques said, taking a healthy swig from his beer bottle.

"I don't know whether this is what you are waiting for, but I give you permission to move on," Hamish said. Jacques' eyebrows knitted together as he looked up to the man. "I don't know what's been holding you back, but if it's Glass... It's well past time you moved on."

Now that he came to think about it, Jacques hadn't actually dated anyone since he'd been sent to prison. When he had been released, he'd hoped that he and Glass could continue from where they left off, but she had vanished. Not even Hamish had known where she was. Since then, he'd had a few one night stands, and his crush on Venom, but he'd made no attempt to actually date anyone. Maybe Hamish was right, and he was subconsciously holding out the hope that maybe Glass would come back to him.

"I'd never thought of it that way," Jacques said absent-mindedly, as he stared at the bottles behind the bar. "Have you seen her since she got back to Seattle?"

"Only briefly. She was just leaving the bar as I got back. I got a quick hug and an 'I've got to go' before she was out the door," Hamish said sadly. There was a pang of guilt. Jacques blamed himself for Glass ditching her Father.

"So you saw the chrome?" Jacques said.

"Oh, yeah, from what I've heard, it's not the first. She's visited Dr. Silver and quite a few of the black market surgeons in the last year," Hamish explained. "I'm concerned she has an augmentic addiction."

"Shit. What the hell happened to her, Hamish? She was always rough and ready to brawl, but this is not her at all," Jacques said. He could feel the concern in his chest. Hamish was right; he was sitting and hoping the girl he had loved would come back to her senses.

"She fell in with the wrong crowd, Jacques, that's all there is. I'll be here waiting when she comes back. Like always," Hamish said; that sad smile was back on his face. "But you aren't going to be waiting with me, are you?"

"You kicking me out? I've still got half a beer left," Jacques said, trying to make light of the serious conversation they were having. His jest got him nothing but a clout around the ear from Hamish.

"You're such a smartass," Hamish said with a chuckle.

"It's just naturally ingrained. Nothing I can do about it, I'm afraid," Jacques said as downed the rest of the beer. "You're right, though, I gotta move on. I'll see you later."

Logically, he should have stayed and waited to see Ava, but his mind was a jumbled mess of emotions. He knew that he had to move on because it was the healthy way to respond to this situation, but he really needed to set his mind straight before he could even consider it. There was no way he could embark on a relationship with someone else until he was entirely sure he was ready. It was only fair. He stepped out of the bar and turned his collar up against the rain. He wasn't sure where he was going, and that just seemed like a metaphor for life right now.

*****

Ava had decided that as Seattle was her new home, it was about time that she actually tried to settle in here. Other than the sets of clothes and toiletries Hamish had provided and the sewing kit she had requested, she didn't have any possessions. Everything she had brought from The Fringe had been trashed apart from her nine mil pistol, but that had to be hidden as it wasn't registered. It was about time she got herself some personal possessions and the first few items to start her business. A few yards of fabric and some embellishments to add to the aesthetic would set her up nicely.

Hamish had shown her how to plot the route on the Silver Bullet Buses, and before she had known it, she was stepping on the bus to Seattle Central. She was surprised to find herself both exhilarated and nervous about the journey. All these years she'd never really been outside the six streets that were the Valkyrie's territory, and since her arrival in Seattle proper, she hadn't strayed far from the Oaken Casket. The bright neons that she had spied over the wall were now within reach, and the thought of seeing them up close excited her more than she expected. This would be her first independent step towards her new life, and she relished the freedom.

When the bus came to stop at the Seattle Central shopping district, she nearly didn't get off the bus.

Recycled Lives

There were so many people. Throngs of people moving about the series of shops and food stands. There were more people shopping today than she'd seen in her entire life. With a deep breath, she'd forced herself to get up and off the bus. She had never been afraid of the general public before, and she wasn't going to start now. Her pride wouldn't let her. Besides, there was no way she'd make it here if she couldn't exist outside the Oaken Casket. What would Jacques think if she couldn't go out to places? Not that that mattered, no, not at all.

The rest of her evening had been taken up by perusing the fashions on offer in the shops, searching for the best places to buy the materials she needed for her clothing, and watching all the people parade around in their own styles. The main contrast seemed to be between the straight cut business attire of smart suits and skirts, and the more haphazard militaristic inspired getups. Both styles seemed to try and show off the person's perfect features as much as was acceptable.

However, her favorite part of the whole experience had been the food court. The place was done up like an indoor market with vendors lined up in neat rows flogging their produce with AR adverts and enticing samples. The sheer choice almost overwhelmed her from sweet snacks to delicious savory delicacies. It had been a nice way to spend her money and her free time, and she left burdened with several bags of items for her to enjoy later. In The Fringe, most of her earnings had gone to the leaders who provided what the women needed and pocketed the rest for themselves.

As she got off the bus and started to walk back to the bar, she started considering the rest of her evening. She was planning to take her purchases and have a few drinks in the bar before bed. Maybe she would even message Jacques and see if he wanted to join her. It would be nice to have a friend for a little while.

She was suddenly distracted from her thoughts by a movement out of the corner of her eye. Her entire body went stiff and her hand drifted to her hip where her gun should be. A small spike of panic went through her when she remembered it was back at the bar. She steeled herself. She didn't need her gun. She could fight just as well without a weapon. She stopped and glanced back over her shoulder slowly. A black cat jumped from a trash can and bolted across the road. She took a deep breath and chuckled at her own nervousness.

"My, my, my, what do we have here?" said a voice with a strong accent. Ava's head snapped back to see Glass standing only feet before her.

"Can I help you with something?" Ava said with an annoyed sigh. This woman was getting on her nerves.

"Yeah, actually, want to tell me what you are still doing here?" she asked, crossing her arms over her chest.

"I am walking home," Ava responded dryly.

"I thought I told you to stay away from the Casket," she said. Ava quirked an eyebrow. She was sure that she had only been warned to stay away from Jacques.

"Actually, you told me to stay away from Jacques, which I didn't do by the way," Ava said with a smirk. She wasn't scared of this girl; she was a head shorter than her for a start. "Shared quite a nice night with him last week."

Glass went a color of red that Ava had never seen on another human being. She almost expected steam to come pouring out of her ears like you saw in a children's book. From the shadows appeared two men, and they flanked Glass like a pair of bookends. Both of them had various patches of chrome, and their flesh parts showed a heft of muscle. Okay, now maybe she was a little out of her depth. She considered calling for backup, but she wasn't that adept with the gauntlet. Glass would know the second she tried, which would just escalate the situation.

"She's mine, boys," Glass said as she rolled up her sleeves, showing off the well-shined chrome arm.

"I'm not afraid to fight you," Ava said as she tossed the shopping bags to one side.

If a throwdown was all this woman needed to back off then that was what she was going to get. As long as those two chromed monster men didn't get involved, then she was going to be fine. The look that Glass had in her eyes was one of a predator stalking its prey; her hands were balled into fists, and she was ready to fight.

"You will be when I smear you on the sidewalk," Glass sneered.

Glass's first attack was easily anticipated. She hit out with the metal arm. Ava got her arm up to block, but it didn't stop the slight pain from the heavy impact of the metal. It was like she had inbuilt knuckle dusters. God, didn't Ava wish she had brought hers with her. She was going to have to be quick and calculated, or else this was going to hurt.

Ava dodged to the side, striking out hard and fast. She caught Glass in the cheek. The weight of the impact caused Glass' head to snap to one side. A surge of adrenaline shot through Ava, the sting in her knuckles reminding her of the thrill of the fight. She was on the balls of her feet, waiting for Glass to respond.

Glass' head turned slowly to look at her. A fury burned in her eyes like Ava had never seen. If anything, she would say there was a sense of crazy in those eyes. It seemed the punch had hit its mark both physically and mentally. The two men in the background started to inch closer. Glass threw out her hand, and they jumped back.

Glass struck out again, and Ava wasn't ready this time. The shot bypassed her guard and caught her in the chest. The hit was so much harder than it should have been, it forced the air from her lungs, winding her for just a second. That augmented arm was damaging. Now she was angry. Who the fuck did this bitch think she was to come start a fight with her? Glass was messing with the wrong girl.

Ava attacked. The combat became a flow of punches and blocks, pain blossoming in one place before quickly being replaced by damage in another.

Recycled Lives

Ava hit, Glass blocked, Glass hit, Ava blocked. Ava was glad that this woman was obviously not much of a fighter, otherwise, she'd make better use of that arm, and that would've made her lethal.

Her knuckles were split, and she tasted blood in her mouth, but that was nothing she wouldn't come back from tomorrow. Feeling confident that she had this in the bag, Ava threw her leg out and swept Glass' legs out from under her. The petite redhead hit the ground hard, and she could hear the air rushing from her lungs as she hit the ground. The two men looked aghast as they seemed to try and decide what to do.

"Want to call it quits now?" Ava asked, breathing heavily from exhaustion. This wasn't exactly the end she had planned for her shopping trip, but it was what it was.

"Quits? This isn't finished, street bitch," Glass sneered.

With unimaginable speed, Glass was back on her feet, and before Ava could get her block up, a heavy punch hit her chest. The pain forced her to back up a little. She grabbed her chest, fighting for breath as another quick blow caught her in the kidney. How had she gotten behind her? Glass' movements were suddenly so quick that she couldn't keep up.

Blow after blow connected with her already battered body. She raised her forearms to try and protect herself from just one attack, but she just wasn't quick enough. What the hell was happening? Had the woman just been feigning before? Ava took a chance throwing a punch that should have caught Glass in the stomach only for it to just graze cloth. The movement opened her up to a blow to the shoulder.

A heavy kick to the back of the knee forced her to the ground, and pain exploded through her knees as she hit the hard sidewalk. No, she couldn't let this woman take her down. She went to push herself up when a heavy black boot connected with her face. The strength of the hit forced her flat out on the ground. She lay there on the ground gasping for breath. She was channeling all her remaining strength into her arms and legs. She needed to get to her feet.

"You're just not going to stay down, are you?" Glass said as she crouched down in front of Ava. Ava could barely make out the boot before her. Her eye was already swelling shut.

"No!" Ava said.

A surge of energy rushed through her as she lurched forward. She grabbed Glass and pushed her to the ground. Glass overbalanced and fell onto her back. Ava didn't have the strength to get to her feet; instead, she grabbed Glass' right leg and sank her teeth in deeply. If nothing else, Ava would leave her mark on the woman. Glass shrieked before kicking out and catching Ava square in the face. There was a sickening crack and an explosion of blood as Ava's nose broke.

That was it. The combination of pain, shock, and multiple injuries was too much. Ava's energy gave out, and she slumped to the floor. The pain emanating from her face was intense, and with the battering the rest of her body had taken, she wasn't sure she would ever be able to move again. That was as long as Glass didn't kill her here and now.

"You know that not all augmentics are visible, right?" She tapped her head. "Adrenal gland enhancement—you'll never beat me, bitch. Now. I'll tell you again. Stay away from Jacques, stay away from my Father, and stay away from the Casket. This is just a warning; if I catch you near there again, I will kill you!" Glass sneered as she knelt over Ava.

When Ava didn't respond, Glass grabbed her long hair and pulled her head up. Ava was forced to meet her eyes. The look on Glass' face was nothing short of psychotic.

"Did you hear me?" Glass asked.

Ava nodded. She wasn't sure she could even manage words right now. But as she heard Glasses' footsteps retreating, she vowed to herself that she would have her revenge. She lay there on the sidewalk, her body broken, bleeding, and bruised, but she would heal, and she would make sure that Glass paid for this.

Chapter Ten

Lucinda had had a lot on her mind since her issue with Sawyer. Zane had talked to her about the issue, and Sawyer had apologized, but Lucinda couldn't help worrying that the girl was mad at her for telling Zane. Sawyer was so quiet all that time that Lucinda had a problem sensing her mood or what was on her mind. Every time Lucinda had been in the house since, she had kept her stuff tucked away in Zane's room just in case. The kids never went in there unless they were invited.

Today had been a hard session at the gym. At least one day a week, she made sure she worked out with Zane. It was useless learning all of the self-defense skills if her body wasn't strong enough to use them effectively. The training was hard, but there was always a sense of euphoria when she was done. With each week that passed, she could feel herself growing stronger. There was the added plus that she got to watch Zane workout while she trained. She would never that turn down.

As they reached the doorstep, Lucinda couldn't help but wonder what they were going to find when they stepped inside. In the few short months since she had been dating Zane, she had walked in on a mixture of compromising moments involving the various members of the family. The twins desperately trying to fix a mirror that they had broken when fighting, Blair plaiting all the boys' hair, Caspian watching adult channels on the main room's AR; that last was one that was sticking with her against her will. Caspian either had very interesting tastes or was really curious.

Zane walked up to the stoop, scanned his chip, and headed inside. He was so used to the craziness in the house that he didn't even falter. Lucinda followed inside more cautiously. There was no screaming, which meant either today was a calm one or everyone had died. In the living room, Caspian and Dare were sitting on the couch watching some cop show on the AR. Zane clapped Caspian round the back of the head. The teenager exclaimed a little at the sudden pain.

"What' chu do that for?" Caspian asked, rubbing the back of head.

"I'm sure I'll find a reason," Zane joked, holding his fist out. Caspian bumped it.

"Morning, Luce," Caspian said.

"Morning. Did you have a good night?" she asked, perching on the edge of the couch.

"Yeah. Went out into town, played some laser tag before picking the kids up. They need feeding, by the way. Zane said I could only order them pizza once a week, and I already did that twice," Caspian said.

"Damn right. They deserve to eat well," Zane said. "I'll take a shower, and then I'll cook dinner."

"It's alright, I've got it. I took a shower at the gym," Lucinda said.

"You sure?" Zane asked.

"Yeah, it's no problem. Caspian and Dare are going to run down to the shop for desserts, ain't you?" Lucinda said, smiling to the boys.

"We are?" Dare asked.

"Yeah, you are. Head down to Tayvian's and get something sweet for us," she said, holding her hand to Caspian. As he clutched it, she transferred him some cash. She then whispered, "There's even a little left for you to get something for yourself."

"No problem, Luce," Caspian said, eagerly getting to his feet. The two young men basically ran out of the front door.

"You spoil them." Zane chuckled from the staircase.

"I can't help myself. When I come back, and the living room isn't a warzone, they deserve the reward," Lucinda chuckled. She put down her workout bag and headed for the kitchen. "Now go and shower, you stink."

Zane laughed again and headed up the stairs. As she stepped into the kitchen, she jumped a little as she saw Blair sitting at the dining table in the kitchen. The littlest member of the family was sitting so quietly that she hadn't even noticed she was here. She had assumed she was either in her room or out playing in the yard.

"Good morning, Blair," she said with a smile as she sat down next to her at the table.

"Lucy," she said excitedly, jumping up to hug her. Lucinda pulled the six-year-old onto her lap and gave her a hug.

"Are you doing your homework?" Lucinda asked.

"No. I finished that, I was drawing a picture," she said, pointing to the AR screen she had been using the paint program on.

"Can I see?" Lucinda asked.

Blair nodded enthusiastically as she turned the AR screen to Lucinda. The picture was of a group of people standing in front of a house with a big green garden and a big yellow sun. Lucinda had an idea of who this was, but she wasn't the artist, so she better clarify.

"That's lovely, Blair. Who are the people?" Lucinda asked.

"Well, this is Vincent and Ryker. They are arguing over a snow cone. Dare and Caspian secretly drink beer when they think Zane isn't looking. Here is Sawyer, she's being all moody on her own over here, and that's you and Zane watching over all of us," Blair said proudly as she pointed out each member of the family. Lucinda felt moved that she had made it into the family portrait that she had drawn.

"Where are you, Blair?" she asked, trying to hide the slight lump in her throat.

"I haven't drawn me yet. I was gonna do that next," the child replied.

"It's an amazing drawing, Blair; you have a real talent. Maybe someday I can show you all my paints,"

Lucinda said with a smile. The thought of teaching her how to paint with oil paints and watercolors thrilled her. She couldn't wait to share her passion with the little girl who had stolen her heart.

"You can? When?" she asked excitedly.

"Not just yet, but I will. I promise," Lucinda said.

"Please, don't go away," Blair said suddenly, wrapping her arms around Lucinda tightly.

"Blair, why would you think that I would go anywhere?" Lucinda asked with a slight chuckle.

"Zane is worried you will. I heard him talking to Cas," she said as she snuggled back into Lucinda.

"Don't worry. I have absolutely no plans to go anywhere," Lucinda responded, kissing the top of Blair's head.

"Okay. Are you going to come and live with us all the time?" Blair asked. The question seemed so innocent from the six-year-old's mouth. It would be so easy to tell her yes, but the decision was so much more complicated.

"I don't know yet. Why? Do you want me to live here?" Lucinda asked.

"Yes. If you are here, then Zane won't be so sad and cross all the time. He's always happy when you're here," she said completely innocently as she played with the ends of Lucinda's short hair. "Also, if you live here, we can get a chocolate fountain in the garden."

Blair's statement confused Lucinda. She struggled to recall any mention of a chocolate fountain in any of their conversations. She was a little worried that maybe she had made a promise to the young girl, and that was certainly something that she didn't want to break.

"So why does me living here mean you can have a chocolate fountain?" Lucinda asked, eager to hear what story the little girl was going to come out with.

"Well, if you ask Zane, then he won't say no," Blair answered innocently.

"Well, I can't promise that will happen," Lucinda responded. She was sure there was no way she could convince Zane that that permanent fixture should be a thing. The kids had enough energy and really didn't need full time access to sugar.

"Oh, okay. Well, when you get married can I be your bridesmaid?" Blair asked.

"Thinking a little ahead there. Now cheer up and go and play with your brothers while I make dinner, okay?" Lucinda said, trying to subvert that conversation as quickly as she possibly could. That was something she certainly wasn't explaining to the six-year-old.

She watched with a smile on her face as Blair nodded and went running out of the kitchen. The little girl's sentiment really filled her heart. She was overcome with a happiness and a sense of belonging that she had never really felt. Originally, she had worried how each of Zane's siblings would take to her. They were a very close family, and she was sure they wouldn't have liked the interloper, but she had been wrong. Pretty much from the first day, the kids had been nice to her. The younger ones mainly. It had taken her a couple weeks to win Caspian over, and she was still working on Sawyer.

She was glad that she was being seen as part of the dysfunctional little family. Even though only a short time had passed, she couldn't imagine what she would do without them. With a smile on her face, she went to the fridge and started gathering what she would need to make dinner for her little tribe.

Chapter Eleven

Jacques had been walking for hours; God only knew how far he had wandered. By the time he'd gotten back to his flat, his feet ached, and he was soaked to the skin. He'd taken a quick shower and settled into his bed, hoping that a good night's sleep would help to wipe the slate. Hopefully, it would banish all of the difficult emotions that had been rattling around in his head all day. He was just drifting off to sleep when he was disturbed by a notification from his gauntlet. He was tempted to ignore it, just roll over and sleep, but something told him that he should check it. An uneasy feeling twisted in his gut.

::Need you down the Casket ASAP::

Jacques sat up, his eyebrows knitting in confusion as he looked at the message from Hamish. Hamish never summoned Jacques, not unless it was important. He sent a reply asking what was up, so he could prepare himself, but when he got no response, he threw himself out of the bed and pulled on some clothes. He checked for messages once more, but when he saw nothing, he headed out of the apartment, slamming the door behind him.

Normally he would just take the bus or walk as it was cheaper, but today he opted to take a cab. He was more concerned about speed rather than the contents of his bank account. He was on the edge of his seat the entire ride as his brain walked through every scenario that could have happened to have Hamish summon him like this. His stomach was twisting and turning with anxiety as the possible outcomes became more and more ridiculous.

When the cab stopped outside the bar, he paid the fare without even looking at how much it was. He was on the way down the steps before the cab had even had a chance to pull away. He was analyzing every detail of the place to try and figure out what had happened. The guards were on the door, and no sign of Seattle Security, which meant it wasn't a raid.

"Morning guys," he muttered to the mercs on the door without stopping.

As he stepped inside the bar proper, he looked around, seeing a few of the regular clientele, but other than that, it seemed relatively quiet. No out of control bar fight. That was another one ticked off the list. The longer it took for him to find out, the more serious it seemed to get in his head. He stepped up to the bar. One of the younger male staff, Keith, was manning the bar solo at the moment.

"Y'alright, Keith? Where is Hamish? He called me." Jacques said, forcing himself to remain calm. He didn't want to seem anxious or on edge.

"Yeah, he's out the back. Go on through," Keith said.

"You know what's going on?" Jacques asked as he headed towards the door.

"Just get back there, man," Keith said as he picked up a glass to fill.

Jacques shook his head as he made for the door to the back room. All of the staff of the Oaken Casket knew not to spread information of anything that went on in the venue. The clientele paid for the privacy, and most of them for good reason; a lot of hidden demons and life destroying secrets were hidden in the walls. His past was light and airy fairy compared to some of them.

He pushed the door open, a cool breeze coming from the stores raising the hairs on the back of his neck. Part of him was expecting to find a dead body wrapped in tarp and Hamish waiting for him to help move it. When it came to this place, there was little that could surprise him.

"Hamish, you here?" Jacques called out.

Hamish appeared from the back storeroom, a look of worry on his face. That concerned Jacques even more; the man wasn't known for showing his concern much. That was when Jacques knew something bad was happening.

"Gonna tell me what's going on?" Jacques asked.

"Now you're here, yeah. It's Ava; she's hurt," Hamish said. Jacques' stomach dropped; what the hell had happened? Had one of the mercs got handsy, maybe one of the punk kids from one of the gangs? He was equally worried and angry. He was already plotting how to hurt whoever had touched her, and maybe that was a giveaway to how he really felt. Then a cold fury rolled over him. Glass. He should have thought of her first.

"Why are you calling me and not a damn medic?" Jacques asked angrily as he headed towards the back room where Ava was living.

"Cause she won't come out, and isn't answering the door. Thinking that you might actually be able to get through to her," Hamish said as he followed closely behind him.

"How hurt is she? What the fuck even happened?" Jacques asked. As he reached the corridor to the bar's private rooms, he saw Sherrie, another member of the bar staff, standing beside Ava's door.

"I was working when she came in. She was a beaten mess. I don't know how she was even walking. I tried talking to her, but she ignored me," Sherrie said with concern in her voice. The staff here were hardy and could take a lot of shit, but it affected everyone when one of their own got hurt.

"It's alright, Sherrie, we got this, you head back to work," Jacques said. The short brunette nodded before leaving. Jacques turned to the door and knocked four times. "Hey, Ava, it's Jacques. You wanna let me in?"

He was greeted by nothing but silence. Jacques glanced to Hamish, who was hanging close by. Hamish shrugged in response.

"Never thought of knocking," he said sarcastically.

Jacques wasn't keen on the idea of breaking into her room. There were some boundaries that they should set. If he wanted a chance at dating her, he needed to show her some respect, but he was also concerned at how hurt she was. Was she not answering because she didn't want to, or was she so hurt that she had fallen unconscious? He knocked more insistently.

"Ava, if you're not going to answer me then I am just gonna come in," Jacques said.

Once again, no answer.

"Okay, I'm breaking in now!" Jacques called through the thick wood.

He sighed as he reached into his pack, pulled out a set of lockpicks, and went to work on the door lock. He'd told Hamish before that he needed to keep spare keys for these back rooms, but the old man was a stickler for privacy. He believed no one but you should have access to where you slept but you. After a few minutes of tinkering, there was a small click as the door was unlocked.

"I'm going to go in. Don't attempt to come in unless I call you, alright? Not sure how she's going to react," Jacques said, his voice a low murmur.

It was weird to be giving Hamish orders, but he really wasn't sure how his intrusion would be received. Ava made him think of a predator, and he was worried that she would strike out when she was wounded and cornered.

"Ava, I'm coming in," Jacques said.

When there was still no response, he pushed the door open and slipped through the gap, closing the door behind him. The sight before him was something he was going to remember for a long time. Ava sat on the cot leaning back against the wall. All visible skin seemed to host a cut or a newly formed bruise, her blonde hair was matted with blood, but the worst was her face. Her nose was obviously broken, one of her eyes was swollen shut, while the other had a deep black bruise. The sheets she was perched on were also covered in blood.

She made no acknowledgement of him entering the room. Instead, she rolled her head back, bringing a mass of cloth to her nose in an attempt to stem the bleeding. Rage exploded within him; whoever had done this was going to hurt more than they ever knew.

"What the fuck happened?" he asked as he moved to her side. He took the cloth from her hand and examined her face; even her lip was swollen.

"Not much, you should see the other guy," Ava said sarcastically.

"Ava, who hurt you?" Jacques demanded.

"It doesn't matter," Ava said, her face creased up in a pained wince. Even talking was hurting her. He wanted to reach out and see where else she was hurt, but he was sure that would not be welcomed.

"It does matter. It matters to me," Jacques said as he climbed off the bed and grabbed a bowl of warm water and a fresh cloth from the sink. He perched beside her on the bed and gently started to clean some of the blood from her face.

"Glass," Ava said.

His blood ran cold at the mention of her name. He hadn't taken the threat seriously. Glass was a brawler of opportunity, not someone to actively seek a fight. She didn't have a vindictive streak. He looked over the injuries that he could see. He didn't even think Glass was able to inflict this sort of damage. What had happened to her? Why the hell had she gone so far off the deep end?

"I told her to leave you alone," Jacques said.

"I guess it didn't work. Seems like your ex ain't over you," she said with a slight chuckle, which quickly turned into a grimace.

Guilt floored him. This had happened because of that stupid date. Glass must have seen them in the diner together. Maybe seen them holding hands as they dashed through the rain. The mixture of emotions from the other night were fading, and he was quickly seeing how he truly felt about the two women in his life. Glass would always hold a small part of him, but Hamish was right. He had no future with a girl who could do this.

"Okay, we've got to get you to a doctor. Some of these wounds are deep and need stitches," Jacques said as he uncovered a rather nasty gash on her wrist.

"I'll be fine. Just need a sewing kit and some thread, and I'll be fine," she said.

"Ava. Please. I'd really like someone who has a medical degree to look over them," he said. He was considering where the closest free clinic was.

"No. I don't want to go to those hospitals. Don't like them," she said with a grunt as the cloth brushed over her bloodied and broken knuckles.

Jacques was starting to feel a little frustrated. All he wanted to do was help her, and she was being stubborn. Now he knew how Hamish had felt all the times that Jacques had turned up here hurt and had to call the medic. That's when an idea stuck him.

"How about I bring a doctor here? Would that be ok?" Jacques asked.

Ava didn't respond straight away. She seemed to think it over for a moment. Jacques went to prompt her for an answer when she nodded slightly. Before she could change her mind, he summoned Dr Silver's contact details. The backstreet doctor was good at what he did, and he did it cheaply with no questions asked. After a quick conversation and a promise of double pay the doctor was on his way. Jacques sat down next to Ava and waited.

*****

Ava was perched on her cot. The pain from her injuries was making it hard for her to really focus on anything. She'd heard the knocking on the door but hadn't really been able to make out what was being said. Not that she cared. She didn't really want anyone seeing her like this. It was bad enough that Sherrie had seen her on the way in. It wasn't just her body that was broken; she felt useless and weak. Two things that didn't sit well with her. The need to feel strong and invincible had been bred into her. If you looked weak in The Fringe, you ended up dead.

When Jacques had entered her room, she was surprised that she hadn't felt the need to run, hide, or throw something at him. She somehow didn't mind him being the one to see what Glass had done to her; if anything, she was glad he was here. He was sitting beside her. She heard the sound of water tinkling as he rinsed out the cloth immediately followed with a stab of pain as he cleaned another of her wounds. There was so much pain that she couldn't even begin to assess the exact extent of the damage.

She had lost that fight. Not just a little, but epically. She kept telling herself that if it wasn't for Glass' augmentic enhancements then she would have won, but that just felt like she was reaching for excuses. She was already thinking what her plan for the next attack would be. Even with this beating, she wouldn't succumb to whatever Glass wanted. Ava didn't bend to bullies. She never had, and that's what had got her kicked out of the Valkyries. She'd refused to bend to Big Boss's sexual wants, and that had got her a beating, too, before she got kicked out. *Good times,* she thought sarcastically.

"I'm just going to talk to Hamish. I'll be back," Jacques said.

A spike of panic shot through her. She grabbed his wrist to stop him leaving. She didn't want Hamish to see what Glass had done to her. Glass was his daughter, and Ava was worried that their feud could cause her to lose her place here. She had come to enjoy the comfort of a bed and a safe place to sleep; returning to homelessness wasn't something she was a fan of.

"Don't tell Hamish what happened," she said.

"I have to, love. He needs to know not to let her in here anymore. I promise it's going to be okay," Jacques said. He leaned in and placed a gentle kiss on her forehead.

His hand slipped from hers, and he headed for the bedroom door. As she watched him leave, there was a sinking feeling that things were going to go horribly wrong for her. This wasn't proving to be a very good fresh start. It was quickly starting to seem like The Fringe part two, just they pretended they were better because the conditions and the technology were mildly improved. It was still a harsh world full of thugs and bullies, except these thugs just had access to better food and medical care.

The sound of the door opening caused her to jump. She hadn't even realized that she had fallen asleep. She looked up slowly to see Jacques had come back. She didn't like the look of concern and anger on his face when he looked at her. It was nice that he cared that much, but she preferred the cocky grin he had when he knew he was winding her up.

"Smile. You look better when you do," she said. Even cracking a smile hurt her face, but she needed to see him smile.

"Not an easy thing to do right now," he said gruffly as he sat down next to her. "For the first time since I met you, I need you to not be stubborn about something."

"That'll be difficult, that's kinda my nature," she joked. His serious face stayed in place, not even a ghost of a smile. "What do you need?"

"I'm gonna pack your stuff up, and you're gonna come and stay with me for a bit," he said. It was a statement not a question. She wasn't really getting a choice here, which could mean only one thing.

"Hamish is kicking me out, isn't he?" she said sadly.

"No. We thought it best that while you are healing, we take you somewhere that Glass doesn't know. Once the Doc's been, I'm going to take you back to my place," Jacques said. "Is that okay with you?"

She hated feeling weak and even more hated seeming weak to others. She wanted to be stubborn and say no and stay here at the Casket. But she wasn't stupid. If Glass turned up here at the moment, she would kill her with no issues. She was going to have to fight her pride and accept Jacques' help.

"I don't think I have much of a choice," Ava said, trying to keep the bitterness out of her tone at the caged feeling.

"I'm glad we see eye to eye on this," Jacques said almost chirpily. "Shall I pack your stuff?"

"Go ahead," she said.

Most would hate the idea of someone rummaging around in their things, but it wasn't like she had much. A few pairs of clothes, a pistol, a pair of knuckle dusters. Nothing really big and secretive that she needed to hide from him.

"When's the doctor getting here?" Ava asked. Not that she was desperate to see him, more that she didn't like the silence.

"He said an hour at most, so not long now," Jacques answered.

Jacques' face was tense. Each time he looked at her, she could see the angry tick in his jaw. The anger wasn't pointed at her, she knew that. It was pointed at the person who'd done this. It was like he was reminding himself what had happened to keep himself angry.

He moved around the room, packing her things into a large black duffle. He stopped at the shopping bags that she had tossed by the door after she had dragged her ass back here. Even beaten to a pulp, she wasn't going to give up the few things that she had earned for herself.

"You buy anything interesting?" Jacques asked as he nodded towards the bags. The ghost of a smirk flickered at the corners of his mouth. Clearly, cheeky Jacques was still there beneath the simmering rage.

"Not overly. Clothes mainly, and some sweet pastry things from a bakery... Taylins... Tayvins... something like that," she replied, struggling to recall the name. She had mainly bought fabrics for clothes, but telling him that seemed weirdly intimate; she'd never really told anyone her desires for clothing before.

"Tayvians?" Jacques asked.

"Yeah, that's the one. I tried some samples, and they were amazing. Can I have one?" she asked. She wished she had the strength to get up and get one herself, but there was no way that was happening.

Without question, Jacques fished around in the bag and brought a cardboard box to the bedside. Before he could walk away, she grabbed his wrist and summoned what little strength she had to pull him down onto the bed beside her. He was packing her stuff to avoid her, and she wasn't having that.

"Have a pastry and talk to me," she said, carefully placing the box on his lap and taking one of the little pastries for herself.

"What about?" he asked.

"Tell me what's on your mind. You're walking around here like you're the one that just got the crap beaten out of them," she said, groaning slightly as her ribs started to protest that she was still breathing.

"I hate that she did this to you. All because of me. Maybe I should have kept clear; at least you would be safe that way," Jacques said honestly. He took one of the little pastries and examined it thoroughly.

"Don't think that way. Some things are worth getting hurt for," she said, admitting a lot more than she intended to in that sentence.

Before she could stop herself, or second guess herself, she reached over and gently took his hand. She was pretty sure the feelings she had were reciprocated. If not, she'd pass this off as a moment of insanity when she felt better. His hand closed around hers, and his thumb gently rubbed her damaged knuckles.

"I promised you I wouldn't let you get hurt," Jacques said.

"No one can control the actions of others, and you can't follow me around all the time. How about you promise that you won't hurt me?" she said.

"That's a promise I can keep," he said.

There was a sudden knock on the door. She dropped his hand in an instant reaction. He got up from the cot and opened the door. The person he welcomed inside was a taller man with a long face and short black hair. He wore a simple suit and carried an umbrella against the rain. There was nothing overly spectacular about him, but he held himself like he was the most important person in the room.

"Doc Silver, this is Ava," Jacques said.

*****

Jacques had sat back and watched as the doctor had gone to work. The multitude of injuries were going to take some serious stitching. He was currently fighting the pit of nausea in his stomach combined with the spike of anger that kept rearing its head. Every time he looked at her, he wanted to march to Glass' and…he didn't even know what he wanted to do. He just wanted to make her pay, but at the same time, he couldn't imagine laying a hand on her. Even after everything she had done to Ava.

The guilt was the worst. Even with what Ava said, he couldn't help thinking that this was his fault. A kiss on the rooftops and a few simple conversations had gotten her beaten to a pulp. Maybe when she was healed up, he'd take his leave, get away from Seattle, and get away from here. Then she'd be safe.

"Jacques…," Ava said.

The sound of her voice pulled him from the train of thought. When he looked at her, any thoughts of leaving evaporated. As much as it would be for her safety, he was selfish and wanted to be near her.

"Yeah, you okay?" he asked as he rushed to her side.

"I was going to ask the same thing. You had a far out look on your face," she said. Her voice was a little softer, indicating the painkiller Dr. Silver had given her was taking effect.

"Yeah, I'm fine. I was just thinking," he said, stroking the back of her hand gently.

"Mr. Mette, can we talk?" Dr. Silver asked as he stepped away from Ava. He snapped off a pair of latex gloves and disposed of them in the bin.

"Sure. I'll be right back, alright?" he said, kissing the back of Ava's hand. Her eyes were glazing over as she rolled her head back onto the bed. Jacques chuckled a little as he headed over to Dr. Silver. "How's she looking, Doc?"

"I've stitched up what I can. The injuries themselves are relatively minor, but there are an awful lot of them. Her nose is broken, and so are at least three of her ribs, but she is lucky. There doesn't appear to be any internal damage," Dr Silver explained. Jacques was relieved to hear that there was nothing serious.

"So what's the next step?" Jacques asked.

"You're going to need to acquire some painkillers and antibiotics to see her through. She is going to need a lot of rest and nothing strenuous," he instructed as he went to his bag and started to pack it up. "I will send you over a list of the drugs you will need. If you can get hold of some osteonites, or osteoblast it will speed up the rib repair; otherwise, it's just time and rest."

"Thanks, doc," Jacques said. He held out his hand, and when the doc took it, he paid twice the usual fee as agreed upon. The doctor bid farewell before leaving.

Dr. Silver was a fantastic surgeon, but he didn't hold a medical license anymore, which meant he wasn't able to prescribe the medication. They would have to find a dealer to get the drugs Ava needed. Well, not him, but he was sure Hamish would have someone who dealt in that kind of thing. The man had all kind of contacts.

Jacques went back over to Ava. Her eyes were closed, and her breathing was steady. It seemed the painkiller had knocked her right out. At least with her comfortable, he could get things sorted without worrying about her. First things first, he went out to the bar. Hamish stood there alongside Sherrie and Keith.

"What's the diagnosis?" Hamish asked gruffly as he sipped from a shot of amber liquid.

"She's gonna be okay, just needs some rest and pills," Jacques said as he sent the doctor's list of medications over to Hamish, "You think you can get these?"

"Not a problem," Hamish said as he glanced down the list. "Sherrie is going to give you a ride to your place. Getting her in a cab like that might raise some eyebrows."

"Alright, we'll head out now. Don't want her here any longer than she needs to be," Jacques said. The longer they were here, the more anxious he became, that was something he'd never felt here before. Glass could walk through those doors at any time, and he didn't know what his reaction would be.

"Get moving then. I'll have the drugs sent over to your place later," Hamish said.

Recycled Lives

Jacques clapped palms with Hamish and made for the backroom with Sherrie right behind him. She started grabbing Ava's bags while he went to Ava. She was wearing very little and covered with a bloody sheet. He couldn't take her out of here like this. He grabbed a fresh, thick blanket and wrapped it around her body. It was only now that he realized how small her frame was. She was tall with wider shoulders, which made her seem more muscular than she was. Right now, he could feel how thin her waist was, and he could see most of her ribs. It showed how malnourished she must have been before she arrived in Seattle.

With her wrapped securely in the warm blanket, he carefully picked her up. Her head came to rest on his shoulder. She instinctively seemed to curl into his body, and he pressed his nose into her hair for a moment. The smell of her shampoo reminded the anxious part of his brain that she was safe, and while banged up, she was alive. She was so much lighter than he had expected. He was already making a plan to ensure she was fed up while she healed. As he carried her out to the car, he could feel her breath playing gently on his neck. Even with all the turmoil, his soul felt a sort of peace in this moment.

It didn't take long for him and Sherrie to get Ava and her things in the car and head off towards his apartment. Other than basic directions, there wasn't any real conversation. He was far too focused on everything else that was happening right now to manage any sort of idle chatter. Sherrie didn't seem bothered.

When they got to his place, Sherrie helped him to get everything up to his apartment before she left. They didn't see any of his neighbors, which was good. Carrying a clearly battered, unconscious woman through your door was going to raise some eyebrows. That was the kind of attention that he really didn't want.

Jacques carried Ava through to his bedroom, laid her gently on the bed, and covered her with the sheets to keep her from getting a chill. He then stood in the doorway for a second watching over her sleeping form. Part of him wanted her to wake up so that they could talk some more, but more so, he was glad that she was resting peacefully. After the beating that she had taken, he was glad to not see her in pain.

Satisfied that she was as comfortable as he could make her, he placed a glass of water by the bed with some meds, checked all the windows and doors to make sure they were locked, before grabbing his spare pillow and blanket and heading for the couch. Now that the adrenaline had stopped pumping, he could feel the exhaustion setting in from his very emotionally charged day. He kicked off his shoes and flopped on the couch. He was only just able to pull the blanket into place before he fell asleep.

Chapter Twelve

After meeting one of her training partners for a few drinks, Lucinda had chosen to spend the day sleeping at home. It seemed like a better idea to get her rather tipsy self to the closest bed rather than travelling halfway across the city drunk and ending up lost on the wrong side of town. It wouldn't be the first time that happened. She curled up in her empty bed, wishing absently that Zane was there with her. She always slept better with him beside her. She sighed. She knew internally that she had made the right choice, even if the outcome wasn't the one she wanted. She pulled the sheets more tightly around her and dozed off.

She woke up the next evening with the worst hangover she'd had in a while. She squinted at the AR screen chirping happily at her that it was 6pm. Shutting down the irritating sound, Lucinda reached into her bedside table to retrieve her pre-made cold coffee and packet of aspirin. She downed the coffee in three large gulps and dragged herself to the shower.

Under the hot spray, she began to feel more alive. Once clean and having pulled on some clean clothes, she made her way over to Zane's house. It was his day off, and they had planned to spend it together.

As soon as she opened the front door, she heard a crash and splintering of wood. Her heart started hammering as she reached for her gun; she immediately worried someone had broken in. There was a grunt and a swear followed by the sounds of a heavy blows hitting flesh. With her gun raised, she crept around the corner, trying to see what was happening.

What she found was Zane and Caspian in the living room wrestling in the ruins of one of the end tables. Zane had one hand around his younger brother's throat as Caspian punched him repeatedly in the kidneys. Not for even a second did Lucinda think this was a friendly fight.

"Stop! Now!" Lucinda shouted. Her voice echoed around the living room.

The two men stopped instantly, both turning to the source of the unexpected noise. Lucinda was filled with disbelief as she saw Caspian's already forming black eye and Zane's split lip. She'd heard tales of their fights before but never had been around to witness one.

Zane forced himself to his feet, his breath coming heavy as he seemed to force himself to walk calmly away from the situation. He placed both his hands on the glass of the patio doors; his shoulders were tight and hunched. Caspian planted his hands on the ground and leaned back, but his eyes were trained entirely on Zane like he was ready to go again. Before she could really think, Lucinda moved into Caspian's eyeline.

"Kitchen now!" Lucinda snapped at him, pointing out of the room.

With a noise that was almost a growl, Caspian got up and stalked to the kitchen. There was a thud as he kicked the wall on the way through. With the fight dissipated, she stood there just looking between the brothers' locations with disbelief. She'd heard from Dare and Zane how bad the fights could get; it was the way they had been raised in The Fringe. They responded to each other with violence when they couldn't express themselves or agree.

She decided that it would be best to talk to Zane first. It would be easier to get through to him than Caspian. She approached him slowly. She didn't want to make him jump. She had seen Caspian do it, and it had resulted in the guy getting a punch to the ribs. His fight reaction was very strong, and he would never forgive himself if he actually hit her. The guilt would eat him alive.

"Want to tell me what that was about?" Lucinda asked with her hands on her hips.

"Just a scrap," he said, still breathing heavily. She wasn't sure whether it was because of the exertion and adrenalin, or whether he'd actually been hurt by Caspian.

"Just a scrap? Didn't look like it to me," she challenged. Her heart was still hammering. Seeing the violence between the two guys had really gotten her on edge. She was becoming accustomed to violent situations at work, but not at home.

"Well, if you'd just listen to me," Caspian called from the kitchen.

"Fuck off, Cas!" Zane yelled back. Lucinda could see the anger rising in Zane again, and she couldn't have them restarting whatever feud was going on. She moved to stand between Zane and the kitchen door and pulled up her AR gauntlet's menu.

"Cas, I've dropped twenty bucks into your account. Get out of here for a bit and take Dare with you," Lucinda called through.

There was no actual response, but she guessed by the sound of the back door slamming that Caspian had gathered Dare from wherever he had been hiding and left the property. Now she could focus on Zane and see if she could calm him down properly. She walked up to him and placed a hand carefully on his bicep.

"Sit down, and let me sort out your lip," she said softly. Zane let her take his hand and lead him back to the couch. She grabbed a damp cloth from the kitchen and stood in front of him, dabbing at the blood that was coming from the split lip. "So you going to tell me what you were fighting about?"

"Same old shit: money. He wants money but can't work for it like he did in The Fringe. He was talking about maybe dealing for some cash," Zane said. She could hear the pain in his tone. "I came here to give them a better life, not for him to become a dealer like he would've back there."

"Is violence really the way, though?" she asked. Now that the adrenaline was wearing off, she could feel the shake coming to her hand. Seeing that level of violence had shaken her up a little more than she expected.

Zane didn't answer for the moment. His square jaw was set in a grim line, and there was a slight tick in the side of mouth as he was obviously trying to pick his words carefully. When they'd first started dating, he had a habit of saying exactly what he thought when he wasn't at work. After he'd accidentally upset her a few times, it was something that he'd trained himself out of. She still always knew when he was chewing on an answer, though.

"You going to talk to me?" Lucinda asked with her hands on her hips.

"You know I've tried to curb this. It's just Cas and I...it's how we do things," Zane said.

"That's the best you've got? That's how we do things? Seriously, Zane, can't you just sit down and talk like normal people?" Lucinda said exasperatedly.

"No, because we aren't normal people. We weren't born here, and where we come from, that's how you settle disputes. Cas was seen as a man that side of the wall, and nine out of ten times he throws the first fucking punch," Zane said. He was quickly winding himself up. She wasn't afraid of him because she knew that there was no way he'd set a hand on her. Dare and Caspian were the only two he fought with. He got to his feet and started pacing the room like a caged animal.

"Ok, okay. I'm sorry I said it that way," she said, placing both her hands up. There was no way that they could discuss this rationally if he was agitated.

"When we have kids, it will be different. I won't teach them that fighting is the only answer. It's just how things were back there. It's hard to breed out something that…," Zane was still talking, but Lucinda had stopped listening.

When we have kids. He'd already thought about this? She was currently stuck on the idea of living with him, and he was already considering how he was going to raise their children. She hadn't even considered if she wanted kids or if she wanted to get married. She had kinda assumed that he wasn't in a rush seeing as they still had all his brothers and sisters living with them.

She swallowed hard. It was tough as her mouth was so dry, and a nauseated feeling was quickly swelling in her stomach. She was rushing into this. She was giving him the impression that she was ready for more than she actually was. Fuck. How could she move into this place where violence like that fight was shrugged off in a second? Maybe this moving in was a really bad idea. Did she really want to be around the guys' explosive tempers all the time?

The need to run was intensifying, but she had just got here. What good excuse did she have to get out of here? Nothing, her brain was drawing a blank. She could feel a tightening in her chest as she started struggling to breathe. Zane was looking at her now, his brows furrowing in concern. Before he could touch her, she jumped to her feet.

"Jacques needs me urgently," she lied as she backed away towards the door, grabbing her bag as she went.

Recycled Lives

No kiss. No hug. She literally ran out the door. It wasn't until she was halfway down the street when she realized what had just happened. She had just run away from her boyfriend. Why? Because of an offhand comment about having kids. Was it really that which was bothering her? Her mind was so muddled. She was completely in love with Zane and had been pretty much since she met him. She really couldn't imagine a future without him, but there were just some things that she couldn't cope with, and she didn't know what to do.

She looked back to the house. She couldn't go back. She couldn't tell him what had just happened. Instead, she made for the diner at the end of the street. She'd have a coffee just to calm herself down and then…then she didn't know what she would do. She was supposed to spend today with him, and she wanted to go back and be entirely honest with him, but she wasn't sure how he'd take it. There was a pit of guilt swirling in her stomach. It was their only day off together this week, and she'd run off and ditched him.

As she pushed the door to the cafe open, the scent of coffee and bacon hit her, making her stomach rumble. She took a seat at a table and flicked through the menu. Using the AR system, she ordered a coffee and a bacon sandwich. She placed her head on the table and groaned a little. How had things gone from being so perfect to a complete mess in the space of a week?

"You and Zane fight, too?" Caspian said. Lucinda looked up slowly to find Zane's younger brother standing beside her with a cup of coffee.

"No...yeah...I don't know," Lucinda said, dragging her hand through her ringlets.

"I know my opinion doesn't matter, but all I ask is if you are going to dump Zane, don't fuck him around," Caspian said. Lucinda's head snapped up. There was a protective fire in his dark eyes.

"What! Why do you think I'm dumping Zane?" Lucinda asked. She may have been freaking out about moving in, but she had never considered splitting up with him. She loved him far too much.

"You've been acting very weird the last couple of weeks. Flaking on him and acting distant. Your relationship ain't none of my business, but I don't want to see my brother hurt," Caspian said.

"Trust me when I say I don't want to hurt Zane," she said. She hadn't quite realized how her emotion had showed on the surface.

"He's never done anything for himself. Not really. It's always been about us. Like I said, if you're going to end it, just...I dunno...be nice or something," Caspian said, shrugging his shoulders a little.

Even after they had fought, Caspian was here standing up for his brother. The anger from whatever had caused their altercation had seemed to have passed, and he stood there fighting for his brother not to get hurt, even while he had a black eye forming from the same brother. Having never had any siblings, she didn't understand this bond. If she had ever argued with anyone, she couldn't then talk nice about them five minutes later.

"Caspian, I'm not ending it with Zane. Things are just complicated right now," Lucinda said with a sigh.

"Well, just fuck and make up. It's always worked for me," Caspian said nonchalantly.

Lucinda felt the laugh as it exploded from her. Caspian was such a gem; he always said things so bluntly and to the point. Unlike Zane, he'd never learned to guard his words, and in a way, she hoped that he never did. It was a part of his character that she loved. He may only be nineteen, but he always seemed a lot more grown up.

"I'll keep that in mind, thanks, Cas," she said with a chuckle. "Can I ask a favor?"

"Sure," he responded.

"Don't tell Zane I was here. Let me figure some things out," Lucinda said. All she needed was for Caspian to go back to Zane and tell him that he had seen her hiding out here, and that was going to make things a whole lot worse.

"Don't worry, I won't," he said.

Lucinda got up and hugged him. Caspian wrapped his arms around her without hesitation. Out of all the siblings, he was the one she had expected to struggle to accept her, but he had actually been one of the most accepting once he got used to her. After a few moments, he stepped back. Without another word, he went back to the other side of the diner and settled at his table with Dare. She slipped back into her seat and put her head in her hands. Now she had to figure what she was going to say to Zane when she saw him next.

Chapter Thirteen

Ava awoke to an aching feeling that covered her entire body. She dreaded the thought of moving as she knew it was going to get a whole lot worse when she did. Cracking her good eye open, she surveyed her surroundings. She wasn't in the back room of the Oaken Casket anymore, that was for sure. The bedroom was painted a calming cream color, with an AR overlay of electrical circuits, and the bed she was tucked up in was covered in a layer of gray blankets. This must be Jacques' room. There was a note scrawled on the AR wall.

::There are painkillers on the nightstand for when you wake up. J::

With a groan, she pushed herself into a sitting position. Fuck, did that hurt. There were aches in places that she didn't know existed, and her mind was a little foggy from the high strength painkillers that the doctor had given her. She grabbed the pills that Jacques had left her and swallowed them down with a large gulp of water. Hopefully, that would dull the aching without knocking her out again.

Rather than risking getting to her feet, she relaxed into the bed; she wanted to see the effect that the painkiller had on her before she tried anything. The last thing she needed right now was to get woozy halfway to the bathroom and collapse, especially as she had no idea if Jacques was even in the apartment.

As she settled into the bed, she found herself looking around the small bedroom. Other than the bed, there was only a modest dresser and a night stand. The bed was made up with matching covers, and everything was neat and tidy, but in such a small space, she guessed it was easy to keep tidy. There weren't any AR posters on the wall, just the electrical wire overlay. There were thick, heavy black curtains covering the one window, with a thin seam in the middle that glowed with light. It must be daytime because it was soft—without the harshness of neon bulbs.

When she was satisfied that the pills weren't going to knock her sideways, she slipped to the edge of the bed. She was careful standing up, making sure that her legs could handle her full weight before subjecting them to it. Once she was standing, she made her way carefully to the door. Opening it slowly and quietly, she found Jacques' small living room. He was fast asleep on the couch with a blanket wrapped around him. It was only now that she thought about her state of dress. She looked down to find herself only in her underwear, her beaten body thoroughly on show. Right now, she couldn't care less. Finding where he'd put her clothes and actually getting dressed would take more energy than she actually had.

She left Jacques to sleep and moved as quietly as she could across the living room. She closed herself in the tiny bathroom and used the toilet before stopping at the mirror over the sink. Her face was a mess of dark bruises, and large strips of what seemed to be tape was holding her nose in place. She tentatively touched her nose, and pain emanated from the origin of her touch. She gritted her teeth, trying to hold in the shout of pain, letting nothing but a low moan escape her. This wasn't the first time she'd been in a fight, but this was the worst beating she'd ever received. She thought that once she'd left The Fringe, she wasn't going to have to fight over men ever again. Clearly, she had been very wrong.

Even through all the aches and pains, all she could now focus on was the growling pit in her stomach. The last time she had eaten had been those few small pastries, and she couldn't even remember when that was. With all the energy she'd expelled during the fight, she really needed to eat something. She left the bathroom and padded softly into the kitchen. She went to the cupboards and quietly opened them to see if she could find a packet of chips or a chocolate bar. Anything quick to eat.

"You're awake. You okay?" Jacques said.

She jumped painfully as she turned to see him just sitting up on the couch. His hair was mussed and his clothes wrinkled from sleep. His eyes cast over her with a slight blurriness to them, as if he wasn't quite conscious yet. She flinched, as she suddenly realized what she was doing. She was going through his shit. There was a spike of nerves and adrenaline as she worried about having to fight for going through his cupboards. In The Fringe, touching someone else's stuff could get you shot. She was just so damn hungry that she didn't think. It was a lot harder to get used to the way things worked this side of the wall than she'd thought it would be.

"I'm starving," she said quickly, defending her invasion of his cupboards. Jacques was instantly on his feet and by her side, all sleepiness gone from his expression. He seemed to already be sizing her up and making sure she was okay to be up and about.

"I've only got a few protein bars here. Let me order something. What do you want, pizza, Chinese, Thai?" Jacques said, already summoning up AR menus.

"Pizza, definitely," she said. Since coming over to this side of the wall, she hadn't exactly reached out and tried a lot of cuisine. In The Fringe, the food had been bland and basic, so it was taking her time to get used to all the intense flavor found in most Seattle foods. Pizza had been one of the things she'd quickly fallen in love with. "Did you bring any of my stuff with you?"

"Yeah, it's all in the duffle in the bedroom," Jacques said.

Knowing that food was on the way injected a little extra energy into her. She made her way back to the bedroom and dug stiffly through the duffle until she found some loose clothes. She was careful pulling the clothes over her skin, as the series of stitches and bruises were agitated by the coarse material.

Recycled Lives

As she headed back into the living room, she was overtaken by the scent of hot coffee. That was something she truly loved about living in Seattle. No more watery coffee. Jacques walked up to her and handed her a cup, the warmth seeping into her fingers.

"Thanks," she said simply. "What time is it?"

"Just after two in the afternoon," Jacques said.

"Sorry, I didn't mean to wake up you up," Ava said honestly.

"You're fine. I'm just glad to see you on your feet," Jacques said, and he sat down on the couch with his own drink.

"I think it's mainly the painkillers keeping me up," she joked. She sipped from the cup and let out a small groan as the taste hit her tongue. She doubted she would ever get used to how good a simple coffee tasted.

"How are you feeling?" Jacques asked.

"I've felt better, a lot better. But I'll live," Ava said, and she lowered herself down onto the couch.

"I'm glad. I was worried," Jacques admitted. Her heart swelled at his admission. Just the fact that someone actually cared about her was warming the ice that had formed in her all those years ago.

She looked up to him and gave him a small smile which he reciprocated. They looked at each other for a few seconds. She wanted to say something, but she also wanted to kiss him again. She knew that was a stupid idea, but that didn't stop her wanting to. There was no way that furthering any relations between them was a good idea.

A sudden knock on the door made them both jump. Jacques got to his feet and grabbed his gun as he edged for the door. He pressed his hand on the AR wall, bringing up a camera feed from the front door. They both audibly released a breath when they saw a drone painted in the pizza store colors, carrying a pizza. Jacques opened the door and retrieved the food.

The gooey, greasy cheese on the doughy base was like heaven. Screw all of those beautifully constructed masterpieces she'd seen on late night cooking shows; this was the best food that she could imagine. Between them, it didn't take long to polish off the large pepperoni. They settled back on the couch. With a full belly, the exhaustion was once again settling over her.

"I think I need to get some more sleep," Ava said with a yawn. She felt a little awkward as she wasn't sure whether to head back into his room or nap on the couch and let him reclaim his space.

"You need help getting back to bed?" Jacques asked, not waiting for her answer as he got straight to his feet and offered his hand to her.

"I can walk…just about," she said as she took his hand and got up. "If you want the bed back, I can just take your couch; it's better than anywhere I've ever slept before."

"Yeah, that's not happening," Jacques said with a chuckle. "I want you to be comfortable."

"Well, how about you join me," she said as she turned to take a step towards the bedroom without letting go of his hand.

She knew that she might be making a mistake, but she just couldn't help herself. For the first time in her life, she actually felt like she was living by her rules. No one could choose her path from now but her. At this time, she felt beat up and shit, and all she wanted was the comfort of another person. She didn't want sex; she just wanted someone close who she could rely on when things got tough. Jacques was quickly becoming that person. Not only that, but knowing that spending time with Jacques pissed off Glass made her want to do it even more.

Jacques didn't say anything, but he followed her into the other room. She stripped back down to her underwear before slipping in between sheets. The bed dipped as he climbed in with her. They lay there in the darkness in silence for a few minutes. In the quiet, she could hear the rhythmic sound of him breathing, and a sense of calm swept over her. She hadn't felt relaxed in a long time.

She rolled over, wrapped her arm over Jacques' chest, and laid her head in the crook of his arm. Before she had a chance to worry about how he'd react, Jacques wrapped his arm very delicately around her. Just having him so close made her feel like everything was right with the world—a strange but entirely welcome experience for her. She closed her eyes with a small smile and let herself fall asleep.

Chapter Fourteen

When Jacques woke up, the bedroom was in pitch darkness. With no sun breaking through the gap in the curtains, he knew that night had fallen. His augmented eyes allowed him to see in low light situations, so he could see the room reasonably well with just the hint of neon coming through the curtains. He looked down to see Ava laid out on his chest. Her gentle, calm breaths played over his skin. He couldn't remember the last time he'd had a girl in his bed and hadn't had sex. If anything, it made his time with her so much more special. He could have happily lay here all week.

He looked up to the AR wall and summoned up his messages. There was one from Hamish. It was a simple inquiry about how Ava was settling in, and asking him to come down to the bar when he had time because he wanted to speak to him about something.

With Ava sleeping peacefully, Jacques decided now was the best time to head out and talk to Hamish. Since he'd been this close to her, his thoughts were very much x-rated. Her skin against his was so soft and was fueling a fire within him that hadn't been quenched in a while. He didn't think the beaten and bruised ex-prostitute would appreciate him coming onto her right now.

With that thought in mind, he moved slowly and carefully to extricate himself from her warmth, slipped from beneath the sheets, and grabbed his clothes. He wrote a quick AR message on the wall and put some more pills on the dresser for Ava before getting dressed and heading out. He made sure his apartment was locked, and he had a live AR feed to watch the door, before grabbing a cab and heading down to the Oaken Casket. He was starting to feel like he had moved back in. It had been a while since he was here every day.

It was rather busy in the bar today. A hum of conversation settled over the room like a blanket. Jacques ignored the queue at the bar and headed straight out the back. No one stopped him; it was the beauty of spending so much time around here in his youth. He headed to Hamish's office, knocked, and as soon as he heard a reply, he headed inside.

"I wasn't expecting to see you so soon. I thought you would be spending the day with Ava," Hamish said with a cocky grin on his face.

"She's sleeping, so I thought I'd see what you wanted," Jacques said as he slipped into the seat opposite him. He decided not to tell Hamish about the thoughts that he'd been having. He wanted her so badly, but with everything going on with Glass, he didn't want to risk fucking her life up any more than he'd already done. She was hardly in any condition to engage in anything even if she had wanted to.

"I've done something I never thought I would have to do, but I'm having issues," Hamish said as he pinched the top of his nose. The strain on his face actually concerned Jacques.

"What's going on, Hamish?" Jacques asked.

"I put out a capture bounty on Glass. Thought that if I could get her back here, maybe I could knock some sense into her, y'know get my daughter back," Hamish explained. The pain in his voice was so obvious. "The problem is none of the mercs I trust with this will touch the job, not with her being my daughter. It also seems she's abandoned the house she was living in, so I can't go and see to her myself. Now I have no idea where to turn."

"You want me to go and find her?" Jacques asked.

"Not exactly. I know you have contacts outside this bar, and I want you to use them to find out where she is," Hamish said. "I'm willing to pay."

Jacques hated that Hamish didn't know who he worked for now. The Seraphim Network could help him out for a price, but Jacques was loath to give the man the organization's name. He liked keeping the two areas of his life separate. He could always put the job to the Network himself, or even better, he could ask the friends that he'd made since working there.

"I think I have a couple people that I can ask. I'll get on that today," Jacques said as he got to his feet. There wasn't any time to spare. The sooner he dealt with this Glass issue, the sooner Ava would be safe. "Message me how much you are offering."

Jacques was out of the office and the bar so quickly he was sure he left a vapor trail. All he was focused on was what resources he had that he could use. The first person he was going to talk to was Venom; they would need a good hacker to find out where Glass was hiding out. Next would be Lucy. If he could get her and her boyfriend on their side, that would be a good start. It was strange to him. For years, he'd found himself wanting Glass back, but now all he wanted was to never see her again. It was crazy how one person could change your view on life.

He'd dropped a call to Venom, asking if she was free, and she agreed to meet him for a quick breakfast near the office; as usual she'd been called in early to work and couldn't spare a whole lot of time. He hadn't really seen much of her since he'd moved out. It had been too hard. In retrospect, he was quickly realizing that his crush on her was just one of loneliness and opportunity. She was a lovely girl, a good friend, and a great one night stand, but they would never have worked. She was a workaholic and rarely ever home, and long term, that wouldn't have worked for him. He grabbed a cab and shot across town. In the last two days, he'd used more of his cash on transport than he would usually use in two months. Luckily, his rent was cheap, and his Network salary pretty good.

He reached the cafe in record time. Venom was sitting in the window, cradling a mug of what was probably coffee and flicking through something on her AR. There was no doubt it was her; he'd recognize that lime green hair and pale, heart-shaped face anywhere. He stepped into the cafe and took the seat opposite. She instantly closed her AR and gave him a friendly smile.

"Hey, stranger, where the hell have you been?" Venom asked. Now that she said that, he couldn't actually recall the last time he had seen her. Had he actually seen her since he'd moved out? Possibly not.

"Here and there. Working, mainly," Jacques said, a heavy layer of guilt settling on him when he realized he'd only come to see his friend because he wanted something.

"So what can I help you with?" Venom asked, getting straight to the point.

"I need help finding someone," Jacques said. There was no point beating around the bush. Venom was happy to get straight to the point, and he felt pressured to get this done as soon as possible. He wanted Ava safe. "I can pay you for your time."

"Don't worry about cash; you're my friend. We work in favors," she joked. A small smirk played at the corner of her mouth. "When I move, you have to come and shift furniture."

"Alright, I can get behind that deal," he said, returning the smile. The guilt was settling heavier as he promised himself he would make more of an effort with his friend in the future. He'd gotten so wrapped up in his own head he'd forgotten everyone else existed.

"So who am I looking for?" Venom asked as she opened an AR screen.

"Her name is Crystal Reid, known to most people as Glass. She's Scottish but has lived in Seattle most of her life. Her chip ID is WA:536-11-0482," Jacques explained. He spent a moment recalling anything that might help Venom track her. It was crazy that after so many years he remembered that small detail.

"It shouldn't take me long. Dare I ask why you are looking for her?" Venom asked.

"Uh…she's my ex, and she's been threatening my…my friend," he said. For some reason, he'd almost called Ava his girlfriend. They were far from that level of intimacy, although his heart did almost skip a beat at the thought. He was turning into such a lovesick sap.

"I'm guessing calling security is out of the question?" Venom said, draining her coffee cup.

"Yeah, this is a private matter. I need to deal with it myself," Jacques explained.

"Alright, I'll help, but I'd rather not have to hide a body with you," Venom said with a chuckle.

"It won't go that far. I just need to get her to leave Ava alone, and get her back to her father so he can straighten her out," Jacques said.

"Alright. Well, I have to go back to work. Be safe and remember the Network is always here for its employees," Venom said as she got to her feet.

"I know. Just would rather keep these parts of my life separate," Jacques said as he got to his feet and embraced her. It felt like years since he had. "So when you moving in with Micah?"

"Not sure yet," she said with a shrug. "We only just started talking about it."

Recycled Lives

With a quick goodbye, she left the cafe. He couldn't believe that she and Micah were already considering moving in. Last time he'd seen her, they had just been starting out. They had barely stayed at each other's places let alone considered getting one of their own. He shook his head. This wasn't the time to consider how much he was failing as a friend. He needed to focus on the job ahead and then fix things with Venom.

Now that he had met with Venom, his next job was to talk with Lucinda. He messaged her, telling her that he needed to talk to her before grabbing a cab and heading for Zane's place. It wasn't often that he asked for help, but it was time that he started relying on other people. Usually, he'd barrel in and try and do this on his own, but since working with the Network, he had learned that being part of a team was infinitely more helpful.

*****

After their falling out, Lucinda had gone back to the house. Zane hadn't brought up what happened, so neither had she. There was a part of her that really wanted to talk to him and explain how she was feeling, but at the same time, she didn't want to make things worse. When Jacques called actually wanting help, she welcomed the distraction.

There had been little talk between them as they waited for Jacques to arrive. Zane was in the kitchen preparing dinner for the evening while she had settled on the couch with her sketchpad. Right now, the page in front of her was empty as she just couldn't summon her creative muse. All she could focus on was what to do about Zane. Caspian and Dare had come back a little after her and hadn't said anything to Zane. She hated that she had asked them to keep a secret, but she really didn't want to make things worse between them.

When there was a knock on the door, Lucinda pretty much jumped to her feet and rushed to answer it. Anything to break the awkward silence that had fallen upon the house. When she saw Jacques on the doorstep, there was a look on his face that she wasn't sure she'd ever seen. It was sorrowful but mixed with determination. Jacques was such a confident and cocky person, and she wasn't used to seeing anything but that from him.

"You alright, Jacques?" Lucinda asked as she indicated into the house.

"I want to say yes, but that would be a lie," Jacques said, dragging his hand through his hair.

"Well, how can we help?" Lucinda asked, bringing him into the kitchen where Zane was cooking.

"I should probably start at the beginning just so you understand the whole story," Jacques said.

Lucinda and Zane sat and listened as Jacques explained about his ex and everything that had happened between her and Ava. Lucinda was surprised. They'd been friends for a while, but he had never really disclosed anything about his past. It was like she was finally getting to know the guy properly. Lucinda was also trying to figure out what was going on between him and Ava. He talked about her a lot more animatedly than anything she had seen from in the past and seemed particularly concerned about her welfare.

"So what is it you want help with?" Zane asked, getting straight to the point. She could hear from his tone that he was in a mood. She was sure this wasn't going to go down well as the two of them struggled to get on at the best of times.

"When Venom manages to track down Glass, I need help to catch her and bring her to the Oaken Casket," Jacques said.

"And why do you need support?" Zane asked. Jacques sighed deeply.

"Because the gang that she runs with has a few nasty members. If things go south, then I could do with some back up," Jacques replied.

"So you're suggesting we walk into the gang hang out with you and hope that she doesn't just have us shot on sight? I'm sorry, but I ain't risking getting killed because of your psycho ex-girlfriend," Zane said.

A stunned silence fell between them. Jacques' face was tight with anger, and his hands gripped the stool he was sitting on. If Lucinda guessed right, he was holding back whatever anger was in him right now because he needed their help.

"Y'know what, Zane, I fucking helped you when you were dying. Who the fuck dragged you across The Fringe when you were bleeding out? Who the fuck gave you blood from their own veins?" Jacques said as he got to his feet.

"Yeah, but why did you do it, Jacques? I get the feeling it wasn't cause you cared. More likely you worried about losing your guide and your escape routes. If I remember rightly, you hated me the entire trip," Zane said. Oh, god, Zane was getting himself worked up again, and after her reaction earlier, Lucinda doubted she'd be able to talk him down again.

Lucinda didn't know what to do. The two main guys in her life stood at opposite ends of the kitchen table, with their hands curled into fists ready to fight and a stare between them daring the other to make the first move. Zane had already been in one fight this afternoon.

"Why don't I go in and check the place out," Caspian said from the doorway. Both the guys' heads snapped to see who had intruded into their imminent fight.

"Excuse me?" Zane said.

"If you need someone to infiltrate a gang, who better to ask than me? I understand gang etiquette, I look a hell of a lot weaker than I actually am, and the babes love me. I could lead this woman out so you can get her on safe ground," Caspian said as he leaned against the doorframe.

The two men stood there for a moment. The tension in the air was so thick that you could cut it with a knife. Lucinda thought the idea was a good one, but she wasn't sure Zane would get behind the idea of letting his little brother walk into a gang den on his own.

"You sure you want to do this?" Zane asked, with a raised brow.

"Sure, why not? I'm bored as shit, and it will entertain me for a little while," Caspian said nonchalantly.

Recycled Lives

Lucinda knew how bored the young man had been. In The Fringe, he was able to drink, do drugs, and go out clubbing whenever he wanted, but seeing as he was only nineteen, it wasn't something he was able to do in Seattle. They had tried to convince him to try new things and develop new hobbies, but he wasn't interested.

"You don't mind him helping out?" Lucinda asked with a quirked brow.

"He's his own man and can make his own choices," Zane said. "And, Jacques, I never said I wouldn't help at all. I just think the three of us going into her territory is stupid and risky. She knows you and will smell a trap."

"I'm just trying to stop someone getting hurt. Not like I've had time to actually get a plan sorted or anything," Jacques snapped.

Lucinda recognized that this was as close to an apology as Jacques was going to get. The two men were both highly charged today, and didn't that put her in quite the position. The room was so tense she wasn't sure whether she should say something or whether she should just let them deal with this. Just the tone of the atmosphere was quickly getting too much to deal with.

"Can we stop with the fighting! I've had enough of this shit for today," Lucinda shouted. The room went silent as all three of the men turned to look at her.

"Sorry," Zane mumbled as he went back to dealing with the food.

"Chill, Luce. Just having a shit couple of days," Jacques said.

"It's fine. Just tell us what you know, and we'll do what we can to help," Lucinda said.

She went to the coffee machine and made them all drinks before taking a seat at the kitchen table. This was obviously important to Jacques as he never asked her for anything. She reached out and placed a hand on his, giving him a slightly sympathetic smile. She just wanted to help.

*****

Jacques took the coffee that Lucinda offered and sipped at it. His head was such a mess, and he needed to get things aligned before he did or said something else that was stupid. He'd come over here hoping to get some help, but instead, he'd picked a fight with Zane, and in all honesty, it was the man's help he wanted. When dealing with gangs, he had the experience and the fighting skills to help him confront Glass and her gang. He still wasn't sure that Zane would help. He had Caspian willing to help, but he hadn't worked with the kid and wasn't sure what he was capable of.

Unfortunately, envy was an ugly emotion. He hadn't liked Zane from the start, and he wouldn't admit it to anyone, but it was entirely because he was envious. Zane was the tall, muscular guy that women lusted after and seemed to get what he wanted with little effort. Lucy had pretty much thrown herself into his arms, and with that had come everything the man needed to get his life sorted. Jacques had had to fight tooth and nail for everything he had. Lucky breaks weren't a thing for him, and his dating life always swung from non-existent to overly complicated without stopping at the normal relationship options in-between.

He sighed and dragged his hand through his hair as he tried to work out what he was going to say. Should he apologize to Zane or just leave things hanging? Maybe he should just grab a cab back to his place and check on Ava. He wanted to forget this entire, stupid situation, go back to his apartment, curl up with her, and forget the world. That's assuming that she was actually interested in him the same way that he was interested in her. That was another difficult conversation he needed to plan for.

"What's the plan then, dude?" Caspian asked, dragging him from his own thoughts. He hadn't even realized that the younger man had sat down at the table.

"Right now, I have no idea. Kinda just running off instinct," Jacques said with a sigh.

"Alright then, what we got?" Caspian said. The guy seemed more animated and excited than Jacques had ever seen in their few interactions.

"I have a hacker friend who's currently trying to find out her location. I need to get her from there to a bar called the Oaken Casket," Jacques said. He wasn't sure what Hamish hoped to achieve by dragging her across town for a conversation, but Jacques had to hope that it would work.

"Well, when she finds out, maybe we can send Cas in to scope the place out, find out what it's like," Lucinda suggested.

"I'll go to back him up in case he causes trouble. Won't be the first bar room brawl he's started," Zane said gruffly from the stove.

"Hey, not my fault. I didn't know she was taken," Caspian said defensively.

"She was married to him, Cas; you knew him," Zane said in disbelief. "Don't let your cock lead this time. Medical is more expensive this side of the wall. I don't think I can I pay in blood over here."

Having actually been to The Fringe, what Zane was saying didn't shock or surprise Jacques in the slightest. He was just glad his stay there was short. He'd had a tough life growing up on the streets, but The Fringe had been a whole 'nother level of crazy.

"Okay, off topic, but definitely a story for later," Lucinda said with a chuckle. "Maybe Caspian's junk is exactly what we use to catch her."

"My pure sexual magnetism," Caspian said arrogantly.

"Alright, get down off that high horse. You're still second rate compared to your brother," Lucinda said. Jacques pretty much saw the bubble burst on the kid's face, but he recovered quickly.

"You have to say that. We know the truth," Caspian said, wiggling his brows at Lucinda. Lucinda cuffed him on the back of the head and laughed.

Jacques felt that pang of envy again as he watched the family messing around. He thought he had that once, back before the prison time. When the members of the Oaken Casket had been like this. They all playfully irritated each other, but when it mattered, they all had each other's backs. After he'd gone to prison and Glass had disappeared, it hadn't been the same. The family had broken down. That just about summed up his entire history, really, family leaving him alone.

"Sorry, Jacques, back to planning," Lucinda said.

"Can't really do much more until Venom gets back to us with the location. Then we can plan more in detail," Jacques said and finished the rest of his coffee. "I need to get back and check on Ava."

He bid them all farewell before leaving the house. He really just needed to clear his head, and the memories of the past were really clouding his judgement. The thought that he was going to be standing on opposite sides from Glass, and the fact that he was going to take her down, was messing with him. The thought of betraying her hurt, but the idea of anything happening to Ava hurt more.

Rather than getting a cab back like he'd initially planned, he decided to walk. He needed to get his head together before he saw Ava. There was no way he could have a conversation with her like this. He didn't want to worry her and didn't want her to know what he was going to do. He had a feeling that she may either try to stop him or want to help him, and he wanted neither of those things. His desire to protect her was so strong, the fierceness of it caught him off guard.

The rain started halfway home, and by the time he got there, he was soaked through. Normally, he was meticulous about wearing waterproof gear, but he had been so focused on the situation with Ava and Glass that he'd forgotten it. As he opened the door, he found Ava laid out on the couch watching some cooking show on the AR. Her brows furrowed as walked through the door.

"Did you fall in a pool or something?" she asked as she paused the show and sat up.

"Nah, storm drains run faster than trains," he joked as he stripped his coat. "I'm just gonna change. I'll be right back."

He went into his room and quickly stripped the wet clothing. He was starting to get really cold. He dried himself down and dressed before heading back into the living room. Ava was at the coffee machine, her show still on pause. Moments later, she came up to him and handed him a coffee.

"You're shivering," she said with an air of concern.

She took his hand and led him to the couch before grabbing the blanket and wrapping it around his shoulders. There was something nice about this, the feeling about being cared for. It had been a long time.

"Thank you," he said.

She didn't answer. Instead, she leaned in and kissed him gently, clearly mindful of the various injuries her face still sported. The feeling of her lips on his had been something he'd sorely craved since the rooftop. His moment of heaven didn't last long enough as she pulled away with a small smile turning up in the least injured corner of her mouth. She picked up her coffee and leaned back on the couch.

"Two questions. What do you want for dinner, and what do you want to watch?" she asked, and she started flicking through lists of shows. He was proud that she was already operating the AR with ease.

"You're not going to ask anything else. Like where I have been? Why I've been out so long?" he asked, a little surprised. He thought she would want to know why he ran out today and why he'd come back all wet, not to just ignore the fact entirely.

"Didn't plan to. You don't have to tell me anything. You have your life, and I have mine. As long as you don't mind that I spent my day eating pizza in my underwear while watching shit AR shows," she said with a slight smile.

"Please don't go anywhere," he said with a contented sigh as he leaned back on the couch.

"Didn't plan on it," she said.

He took the risk. He put an arm around her and pulled her so she was leaning against him. He expected her to fight him and pull away, but she didn't. Instead, she snuggled in a little closer and tucked her feet up under her without taking her eyes off the screen. He felt like they had just reached some unspoken agreement. Some acceptance of what they were, without having to have some epic discussion about it, and that was something he was happy with. The less conversation the better. With everything that had gone on today, he was just happy to be here.

Chapter Fifteen

Jacques was dragged from the depths of sleep by the sound of chiming from his gauntlet. With a slight groan, he opened an eye to see who was calling him. It was Venom. With great regret, he unwrapped himself from Ava and slipped quietly out of bed. Unfortunately, this was something he couldn't ignore, and he didn't want to risk waking the woman curled up in his bed. He headed into the living room and settled on the couch before hitting accept.

"Afternoon, V," Jacques said, stifling a yawn. "Do you know what time it is?"

"Yeah, a little after midday," she said with a slight chuckle. "Sorry, I got so wrapped up in work I didn't notice the time."

"That's alright. What's up?" Jacques asked.

"I was calling about that favor you asked. I found her," Venom said. Jacques didn't know why he was shocked. Venom was always efficient, but he just assumed that Glass wouldn't be that easy to find.

"Where is she?" Jacques asked.

"She's in a clubhouse in North Tacoma; seems like the place is run by the Chrome Razors. Pretty cheery looking group of guys," she said sarcastically. "I'll send you through the details."

"Thanks, V. I appreciate the help," Jacques said.

"I'm always there for my friends, don't worry," she said.

Jacques thanked her once more before ending the call. When this was over, he'd make sure they met up for coffee or something, just to catch up on life. He dragged his hands through his hair as he tried to get the plan straight in his head. He'd have to go and see Lucy in the morning and get things together with Caspian. He wasn't sure about sending the kid in there, but Zane seemed confident in him.

"So you're going after her, huh?" said Ava from the bedroom doorway. Her voice was flat, emotionless.

Jacques' head snapped up to see her leaning against the doorframe. She was wearing nothing but her underwear. Her skin was still a canvas of bruises and cuts, but somehow, she was still the most beautiful sight he'd ever seen.

"Yeah. I've got to," Jacques said sadly.

"Look, I'll just get my shit and get out of your way. You obviously still like her," Ava said as she turned towards the bedroom.

"No," he said as he jumped up and grabbed her hand. "No, Ava, I'm going after her so I can get her to leave us alone. I don't want her…I want you, you idiot."

Recycled Lives

The words had come out of his mouth faster than he could construct the sentence. He watched her face for a reaction; a smile appeared in the corner of her lips before spreading across her face. She laughed, and her face just lit up.

"I like the sentiment...and the insult worked well," she said as she walked up to him and cupped his chin. "One thing; don't try and protect me behind my back. I'm a fighter, not a damsel in distress."

She leaned in and kissed him. It was powerful and dominating—totally different from the one they had shared the night before, or the one on the roof. Everything with her seemed like a battle, and that was something he was coming to enjoy. It was more than a bit of a turn on. They both pulled away a little breathless and smiled at each other.

"So you gonna tell me what's happening?" she asked

Jacques took a moment to explain to her the bare bones of the plan that he had been working on with Lucy and Zane the day before. He really didn't want her to be a part of this, but he wondered whether he was trying to protect her or whether he wanted to do this himself to prove to her that he could provide for her. As much as he didn't like it, he was quickly realizing that this wasn't his decision to make. She was the one who Glass had hurt, and he knew she'd seek vengeance on her own if he didn't allow her to help. She wasn't a Seattle girl after all.

"What do you think Hamish is going to do with her?" Ava asked.

"I don't know. But that's up to him, not me. I'm done with her after this," Jacques said. He really wanted her to see that his only interest in Glass was getting her to her father.

"What can I do to help?" Ava asked.

"How about we work on the plan later? Right now, I just want to sleep," Jacques said.

Sleep was the second thing on his mind. Primarily, he wanted to just climb into bed and cuddle up with her. He took her by the hand and led her back to the bed. She came without argument. They settled into the sheets, and he pulled her gently into his arms and enjoyed the way she pressed against him. He took in the scent of her hair and the feel of her skin against his. He ran his fingers ever so gently down her arm and entangled his fingers with hers. His body followed the arch of hers, fitting perfectly around her smaller frame. She moved ever so slightly, and the movement of her ass caused an instant reaction in his cock. Sleep was quickly becoming a distant afterthought as his hormones seemed to have other ideas.

"Jacques…can we not?" Ava said forlornly.

There was a spike of panic as he froze. He hadn't intended to try anything with her, but he doubted that she was going to believe that it was an accidental reaction. She rolled over, and his augmented eyes allowed him to see her clear as day. He was trying to work out what to say when she sighed deeply.

"When I came to Seattle, I promised myself I was done having random sex with people. My entire life I sold sex. I sold myself to people, and I didn't get a say in how my life was run. Now I have a chance to do things that I want. To live the way I want to live, and I guess I don't want things to get complicated. Sex is complicated for me. The long and short is I want to find out who I am before I start having sex again. I don't want to fall back into old habits and end up like so many of the others," Ava explained.

That was one of the most real things she had said to him since they'd started hanging out. The sincerity in her voice was so strong that it made him feel proud in a strange way. He was proud of her for standing her ground and for doing something for her.

"I totally understand and respect that," he said as he leaned in to kiss her. "I didn't mean for it to happen anyway. Stupid thing has a mind of its own and its own agenda to go with it."

She released a breath, and as she did, her entire body relaxed again. It seemed like that was something that had been worrying her. She always carried herself with such a confident and strong persona that it was tough to imagine anything truly hurting her. She had brushed off Glass' physical attack with relative ease, so he had never considered how his involuntary actions could hurt her.

"I'm not saying not ever, just you know, not...now," Ava finished lamely. She looked almost guilty about refusing him. "I just started working out who I can be here. I want to know that before I—"

"It's okay. Like I said—body parts that work to their own agendas. I had no input into that reaction. My brain was set on sleep." He crooked her a half smile, keen to reassure her that he wasn't just interested in sex with her. He felt something shift in his chest, like a part of him realized how special she was and how much he cared for her.

"Would it be bad of me to ask what things were like with the Valkyries? Just to understand what you went through?" Jacques asked. He had been intrigued by her past, but hadn't been sure how to bring it up with her in normal conversation.

"You can't understand if you don't ask," she said quietly. She rolled onto her back and stared at the ceiling. "The Valkyries recruit young. They look after the girls until they reach fifteen, which is when they are trained in the trade."

"So do they take them from their families?" Jacques asked.

"No. The families usually offer them. The Fringe is a harsh place for a child. The Valkyries actually look after the children pretty well all things considered. Kept a roof over our heads, clothed, fed, and defended us, and at sixteen, they offered us the chance to be fully fledged members. The offer of pay for sex is a tantalizing one. You've grown up seeing people make their living that way every day, and there's no telling if you can survive on your own. Most sign up. To be honest, the first couple years were easy; it was good, but after time, it starts to grate on you, and you just want more. Especially given that you don't actually get to keep hold of your pay, and you don't really get a say in what or who you do."

"So was your mom a Valkyrie?" he asked.

"Yeah, I was a typical Valkyrie. Mother was a Valkyrie, Father was a Fringe Rider. I never knew him, and she died when I was six, so I didn't really have any special treatment," she explained. "What about you; what's your family like?"

"God knows," he said with a dark chuckle. "My parents abandoned me when I was a little kid. Literally have no idea who they are or where they came from. I spent my life being bounced around Seattle orphanages until I eventually got kicked out on the streets. I was given the option to find out who they were, but I thought 'fuck it'. They didn't care enough to get in contact, so why should I care who they are?"

When they had given him the option of finding out, there had never been a question in his mind. He didn't care who they were and what their reasons were. They had chosen to abandon him, and that was all that mattered. If he ever got the chance to be a father, then he would make sure his kid knew how much he cared about them.

"Seems like we both had shit starts," Ava said.

"Must be why we get on so well," Jacques said with a smile to her.

With that, she cuddled back into him. Her head came to rest on his shoulder, and her arm wrapped around his waist. He relaxed into her, his fingers playing in her hair. Soon her breathing became calm and steady. She was asleep. Tomorrow would be a tough day. Tomorrow, he would go to Lucy and Zane's and plan to catch Glass. This would all be over soon enough.

Chapter Sixteen

Caspian couldn't believe that Zane had actually allowed him to help out with this job. Since they'd fled from The Fringe, he'd found himself getting bored. Seattle's laws were really strict. He'd already been caught once for underage drinking, and if he got hit again, then the Network wasn't going to be pleased. Seeing as their ID chips were faked, he couldn't bring too much attention to them, or he would risk the family being discovered.

Since then, he'd passed his days just trying to keep himself amused. He'd become pretty hooked on those damn online games, but even that didn't scratch the itch. He missed the adrenaline; he missed the drink and the drugs. Maybe that's why Zane hadn't fought him on this. He must know that he needed the outlet.

As he approached the club house, he wasn't nervous. Gangs weren't something that concerned him. Between his father and Zane, he'd grown up in the gang lifestyle, with the violence, the attitude, the alcohol. He doubted there was anything in here that he hadn't seen before. Add in the fact that the Seattle lifestyle was generally just easier, with more resources available, and the Seattle gangs seemed tamer than those in The Fringe. At least here, killing him came with messy consequences that needed to be hidden, not just dumped curbside for the rats to chew on.

He was dressed in some of his more worn down clothing, his long sandy hair was pulled back in a messy ponytail, and his sleeves were pulled up, showing the mess of tattoos that covered his forearms. All of them were from The Fringe and had been done with old school ink and needle, none of this new age nano tattoo bullshit. Zane had suggested he have them removed, but they were part of him. He'd changed his face a little, but those stayed. All in all, he was trying to look as rough as he could. The black eye that Zane had given him was certainly going to add to the image.

The gang house was in what he had come to know as one of the darker parts of town. He'd done his research on the Chrome Razors. They were known for their augmentations, the name gave it away really, and were one of the less organized gangs. They didn't seem to have a particular income, just general troublemaking and selling stolen goods. He didn't have any augmentations himself and never intended to get any, but he could lie like hell, and that's what he intended to do.

There were motorbikes parked out in front, and on either side of the door were two gnarly-looking guys. Both of them were toting shiny chrome arms and a look that said 'fuck off'. He stuffed his hands in his pockets and approached them.

Recycled Lives

"Where'd you think you're going?" one of the bouncers said, his hand stopping his shoulder.

"Look, man, I just want a drink. My fucking dickhead brother kicked me out. I just need to get fucked up, and I heard this joint was the place to do so," Caspian said in a hard and pissed off tone.

"Fine. Don't cause trouble," the guy said as he let him through.

Relieved that he'd passed the first hurdle, he stepped inside the bar. Luckily, they didn't check his ID; otherwise, they would find out that he was underage. He was just glad that he looked a lot older than he actually was. The Fringe was clearly good for something.

The inside of the building was low lit, music played loudly from one of the speakers, and the AR walls projected images of augmented people dancing to the tune. A hubbud of chatter from the multiple gangers hung just below the volume of the music. He subtly eyed the other patrons as he made his way to the bar. They were all chromed up with at least one piece of obvious augmentics and probably a couple more internal enhancements.

"Beer," he said to the female bartender. She gave him a flirtatious smile before going to get his drink. He placed his hand on the bar and paid the bill, adding a little on top. "Get yourself something, too, darling."

She took the tip and moved along the bar to serve someone else. She was a pretty face, but he had to stay focused on the job, not on where his cock wanted to play. It had been too fucking long since he last got laid. A man shouldn't have to go to bed alone for a month. He leaned on the bar, sipping occasionally from his beer, as he surveyed the bar for the mark. There was no way he could forget her face. Jacques and Zane had made him stare at the picture for what felt like hours. Red hair, pretty face, bad attitude, and an augmented arm. Just his kinda girl.

He finished one beer and had started a second before he caught any sight of the target. She appeared from a side door, which he assumed led to the floor above. She was in conversation with a bigger guy. The pair exchanged a few quiet words before the guy nodded in his direction. There was a stab of concern in his gut. Hopefully, this wasn't him about to get thrown out or worse. Glass nodded and headed straight in his direction. He kept his eyes down so she didn't know he had been surveilling her.

"Well, hello, new blood," Glass said as she took the seat beside him.

"Evening," he said gruffly.

"Am I intruding on your bad night?" she asked sarcastically.

"A little. Just want to get fucked up and forget about my asshole brother," he said as he took a heavy swig from his drink.

"He kick you out?" Glass asked. She indicated to the bartender, who quickly got him another drink and placed it on the bar before him.

"Yeah, said he didn't want to see me ever again," Caspian said. He'd practiced the story in his head multiple times just to make sure he wouldn't trip up. It was unlikely, though; he was good at lying to people.

"Now I need to sell my bike and need the cash to find a new place."

"Well, you came to the right place," she said, resting her hand on his forearm.

Bingo, he thought. That was the movement he wanted, a sign that this sob story was getting him somewhere. A lot of the gangs wanted the same thing, new blood. Whether it was for them to pay dues or that they needed more men in the next gang war they were a part of, all gangs were constantly recruiting.

"You'll be willing to buy my bike?" he said, feigning the excitement. All he needed was her to come to 'look' at it. Then Zane and Jacques could grab her. He just needed to get her as far away from the club as he could manage. He didn't need them calling for backup.

"I ain't looking to buy a bike, but I am looking for some new friends," she said, a slight smirk turning up in the corner of her mouth. "If you want to join me and the boys, we'll give you somewhere to stay, help you get paid, and get you all the pussy that you want."

Fuck, he swore mentally as the bike excuse fell flat. There went one of his excuses for getting her out the club; now he needed to figure something else out. His mind was running at a million miles an hour as he tried to come up with some reason for her to leave the clubhouse. He was coming up blank. For now, he needed to keep her sweet.

"Are you the one offering, cause you are beautiful," Caspian said, and he reached out his fingers, stroking her cheek gently. She didn't pull away, and no one came up to punch him, so that was a good start.

"Oh, you're feisty, aren't you?" Glass said with a husky laugh.

"What can I say? When I see something I like, I go for it, and you…mhmmm…I like," Caspian said as he looked her up and down. She was pretty, but there was some crazy kind of aura that surrounded her. Well, he guessed a lot of girls back in The Fringe were like that, and that had never put him off before.

"I don't normally sleep with the new recruits," she said. She was trying to seem stern and authoritative, but the smirk that took over the corner of her mouth was telling a completely different story. Clearly, she didn't like always playing by the rules.

"But for me, you'll make an exception," Caspian said with raised brows, making it a statement, not a question. This was going completely off script, but if it worked, it worked.

She looked him up and down. The obvious judging didn't bother him; he leaned back in his chair looking cocky and confident. He let her see his toned biceps and inked forearms. When her eyes rested on his crotch for longer than they should, he knew that he was in. He leaned in and took her hand.

"So are we doing this or not?" he asked confidently.

"Alright, but you better impress me," she said as she tried to give some impression that she was still in charge of the situation.

Her hand tightened around his as she led him through one of the back doors of the club. He tried to keep track of the way they went in case he had to get back through here in a hurry. That was unlikely, though. If everything went to pot, then he wasn't going to run back through the bar of heavily augmented men. He was jumping out the fucking window and running for his goddamn life. He could feel the subtle vibrations on his gauntlet; so far, he'd had close to twenty messages from the team outside. There was no way he'd have time to look without arousing suspicion. He just had to hope they would trust him to get this done and not come rushing in half-cocked to 'save' him.

They stepped into a room on the second floor. It wasn't a huge room; most of the space was dominated by a double bed. The rest of the room was neatly organized. A dresser with knick knacks was on one side of the room, and a desk with a backpack was on the other side. Most importantly, there was a window. That was going to be his escape route.

She walked towards the bed with a suggestive wiggle to her hips. She sat on the edge, leaning back with a look of lust burning in her eyes. She leaned back, slowly showing off the long curves of her body. Oh, god, he wished he could take advantage of this situation. He was actually considering fucking her and then getting her out of here. It had been far too long. But he knew that Zane and Jacques would lynch him if he did that.

She beckoned him towards the bed. He wrapped his arms around himself, making it look like he was going to strip his shirt for her, but instead, he grabbed the knockout patch that was in his pocket. *The perfect back-up weapon.* He kept it hidden in his palm as he pulled his shirt over his head. He had to at least make this look real. He approached the bed. A knee either side of her lap, he wrapped his arms around her and pulled her in for a kiss. It was a distraction as he pulled the back off the patch in his hand. He cupped the back of her neck tightly, sticking the patch on as they kissed. Within moments, the knock-out drug on the patch seeped into her skin, and she fell unconscious in front of him.

He gently laid her on the bed and grabbed his shirt from where he had discarded it. He was just glad that he'd had a few of those patches left over from The Fringe. He and Dare had used them for a game where they tried to get each other with them at the worst times. Caspian would never forgive Dare for the time he'd patched him when he had just been about to bed a girl. He'd ended up going horizontal on the bar floor and being mocked by the gang for weeks.

With the shirt back in place, he went to the window and examined the route below. Luckily, it wasn't a long fall, and there was a full garbage bin below him. This should be easy. He'd gotten out of worse situations than this. He grabbed Glass and put her over his shoulders before easing himself out the window. The landing into the trash was louder than he would have liked. He quickly jumped out and ran before someone came to investigate the strange noise.

This was one of the weirdest situations of his life. He was running from shadow to shadow as he carried the unconscious form of a woman. If the cops caught him now, there was no way he was talking his way out of this. The adrenaline flooded his veins as he reached the meeting point. Jacques, Zane, and Lucy all looked to him with confusion as he laid Glass on the back seat of the car they had hired for the job.

"What happened to the plan, Cas?" Zane asked with a warning tone to his voice.

"There was a minor complication. Can we get driving now? I rather like living," Cas said, trying to catch his breath and checking over his shoulder to make sure none of the Chrome Razors were following.

They left quickly, heading for the drop-off point, Jacques and Lucinda in the car with the still unconscious Glass, and the two brothers on the bike. The adrenaline was still making Caspian's heart pound, but so was the lust. Goddammit, he'd enjoyed the rush, but when this was done, he really had to find himself a girl. A month long dry spell was something he wasn't interested in continuing.

Chapter Seventeen

Jacques couldn't believe the job had gone so simply, and he couldn't believe that Zane's brother had been the one to complete it. The guy had gone in and picked her up with no issues. Jacques had expected a bar fight or to have to restrain Glass to get her in the car, but nothing had happened. Jacques looked back to the unconscious form of Glass on the back seat of the rented car. He found himself questioning what had happened to her, and what had made her act the way she had. Lying there on the seats, she didn't look capable of anything severe. He could understand her being jealous, but not enough to beat the living shit out of someone.

"You alright, Jacques?" Lucy asked from the driver's seat. Jacques was glad that the guys had taken Zane's bike at this point, thankful for the privacy to talk to his friend.

"Yeah, just thinking. This entire situation has gotten so fucked up. I've basically kidnapped my ex because she beat up my current squeeze," Jacques said, dragging his hand through his hair.

"You and Ava actually a thing?" Lucy asked.

"Yeah…kinda…I think so…shut up," he said, blushing and pointing at her when she smirked at him. Despite himself, a smile broke on his face. Even amidst all the bullshit, he'd actually found a source of happiness. What Glass had done was mental, but she pushed him and Ava together.

"That's awesome, dude. We can double date," she said with a grin.

"Yeah, let me figure out exactly what's going on first," he said with a slight chuckle.

"I'm happy for you. It's funny to think, we went into The Fringe lonely and single and ended up bringing home our partners," Lucy said. They both chuckled a little.

The cheery mood didn't last long as they arrived at the Casket. Jacques didn't bother to park out front. The mercs weren't happy with the capture. Glass had been like a little sister to most, so he wasn't going to drag her past them. Instead, he instructed Lucy to park out by the loading dock. He messaged Ava and Hamish, and within moments, the heavy metal shutters were pulled up. Both of them stood on the other side. Jacques went to get Glass out of the back of the car.

"Let me do it. She's my girl," Hamish said as he pushed past the others to take Glass from the back of the car. It was easy to forget this was his little girl, the daughter that he'd taught to walk, to talk, to read. The daughter who had gone rogue. "You leave this to me, Jacques. She's mine."

Hamish headed through the shutters, clutching the unconscious form of his daughter close to his chest. The rest of them stood outside a little awkwardly. Everything had come to a head only for Hamish to disappear before they knew what was going to happen next. Jacques turned to Lucy, Zane, and Caspian.

"You guys can head off if you want. I can forward your money from Hamish when he's done," Jacques said awkwardly. He really was lost with what to do.

"I don't want your money, dude. I was helping a friend," Zane said, clapping him on the back. He appreciated the gesture, he really did.

"I do," Caspian whispered as he leaned in close. Jacques couldn't help the chuckle. It started small and grew into a belly laugh. Now that Glass was in her father's hands, maybe he could start getting his life back together.

"Let me get you guys a drink before you go back," Jacques said, leading them into the bar.

"Well, I'll have to take Zane's cause y'know he has to drive," Cas said, wrapping an arm around his brother's neck.

"Yeah, Cas will need the extra beer to keep him warm when he's walking home." Zane smirked as he nudged his brother.

Jacques listened to the brothers bickering, but he didn't care much about that right now. He moved to walk in step with Ava, slowly snaking his arm around her shoulders. When her arm wrapped around his waist, he let loose a small sigh. There were so many things that he wanted to say, but he just didn't have the words right now. Plus, there were far too many people around.

When they got inside the main area, they slipped into a booth at the back of the room, and Jacques ordered them a round of drinks. The conversation was light and pleasant, but he couldn't really focus. All he could think about was what was going to happen to Glass. What was Hamish going to do to fix her? Was anything going to stop him caring about her?

*****

As soon as Glass had been brought into the Oaken Casket, Ava had felt more on edge than she had since she dragged herself in after her beating at the other woman's hands. There was something about her being here that made Ava feel unsafe, not just for her but for everyone else as well. It was like inviting a ticking bomb into the building. Hamish understood what she had done, but at the same time, Glass was his daughter. If he showed her too much compassion and let her go, then Ava was expecting to have to go through round two with her. Seattle's drugs had helped her to heal up reasonably quickly, but she still wasn't sure that she could fight against that augment. She could never be as fast or hit as hard as Glass unless she got enhancements herself.

"Are you okay?" Jacques asked. An hour had passed, and she only just realized that she hadn't really spoken since they sat down at the table. She hadn't noticed that so much time had passed.

"Yeah, I'm fine. Just tired," she lied. If it had been just the two of them, maybe she would have said more, but with the ex-Fringe Rider brothers here, she felt the need to keep her feelings to herself.

Hamish emerged from the back room. The look on his face was one of sorrow, thoughtfulness, and confusion. She may not have known him long, but the intense thinking face was one that she had quickly come to recognize.

"You alright, Hamish?" Jacques asked before she could.

"She's an augment addict. That fucking gang has corrupted her, Jacques," Hamish said, dragging his hand down her face. "They forced her to get that arm to be part of that gang. She has eight augments already, and they are all black market shit. She's only been gone eighteen months! She shouldn't have half as many Augs in a year. She could have psychosis for god's sake. All to fit in with some low life scum."

The group around the table had gone silent as Hamish had started to rant. He was getting angrier by the second. He paced back and forth, his hands curled into fists as his eyes were mainly focused on the floor, but occasionally looking back to the table.

"What does that mean?" Ava asked. She felt like an idiot right now, but she didn't understand much about augmentation. It didn't interest her, so she'd never looked into it.

"Black Market means the implants she have are either 'second' hand from unwilling donors, poor quality, or recalled models. It would explain her attitude change; it could be the start of cyber psychosis," Jacques said as he dragged his hand down over his face. She could see the concern there.

Jealousy was starting to bubble up in her. Through everything Glass had done, he still cared about her. How could she ever compete against that? She had opened herself up to him, and she had done it knowing it was probably the worst mistake that she was ever going to make. She took a deep breath, trying to calm her racing thoughts. The jury was still out on that. Just cause he cared didn't mean he was going to go running back to her.

"What's cyber psychosis?" Caspian asked. She was just glad he did so she didn't have to.

"It's when someone gets too many augments too quickly, or when the augments aren't properly made. People who got prototypes back in the beginning were prone to it," Hamish explained. "I'm gonna have to get her to a shrink. We need to investigate the implants and find out what the hell she has had done. Fuck, that girl has a habit of getting herself into trouble."

"Tell me about it," Jacques said.

Ava sat there, not entirely sure what to say. She'd come all the way to the other side of the wall to meet a guy who was still in love with somebody else. Her life was a mess. She wanted to finish her drink, say her goodbyes, and get some space, but all her stuff was at Jacques' apartment. She couldn't even escape this one easily.

Recycled Lives

Before she could figure out what she was going to do, the door to the Oaken Casket slammed open. The noise was so loud that all the patrons of the bar turned to see the source. One by one, a line of gangers started down the stairs. Each one had at least one chrome limb, and they dressed in leather and shiny silver clothing. Ava felt pretty sure these were the Chrome Razors, and the name seemed to fit.

Hamish straightened as he saw the new people in his bar. He glanced sideways to Jacques before heading forward and going almost chest to chest with the leader of the column. Ava was analyzing the body language. The gangers' shoulders were tight, and their faces were set. They were prepared to attack. She looked over to Caspian.

"Under the table now," Ava demanded quietly.

The kid didn't even question the demand. Taking his drink with him, he slid down, disappearing beneath the booth. Lucinda and Zane slid closer to disguise the gap that had been there before.

"Hello, Gentlemen, how can I help you?" Hamish asked, using his kind proprietor voice.

Ava looked across the bar to Sherrie and Keith. Both of them were watching the group with concern. *Look at me*, Ava thought. The two of them were standing there like rabbits in headlights. Fuck! She really regretted her position right now.

"Help us? Well, you can give Glass to us now, and then we'll be on our way," the lead guy said, sneering. There were two silver teeth on one side and one missing on the other. She was starting to wonder whether she hadn't left The Fringe at all.

"Glass? We have plenty of them under the bar; how many do you need?" Hamish asked facetiously.

"You know who we are talking about, old man. We tracked her to the alley," the lead man said, obviously becoming annoyed.

Jacques was on edge next to her. He had a pistol on his belt, but that wasn't going to offer enough of a threat to make them leave. There were a couple of shotguns under the bar, and they would make a lot more of an impact. She was now glad they had chosen the booth tucked away in the corner. Everyone was focused on the action in the center of the room.

She slipped out of her seat, using the shadows as cover to move across to the bar. She slipped through the hatch on the bar. Keeping low to remain out of sight, she moved to the first of the concealed weapons; they were meant for moments such as this. The tight cylinder choke shotgun would do exactly what she needed. She carefully and quietly popped it out of its hold. She knew for a fact that it was already loaded and well maintained. Hamish insisted on it.

"I have no idea what you're talking about," Hamish lied. She knew he wasn't going to give up his daughter that easily.

"I will kill you if you don't tell me where she is," the lead man said, anger dripping from his voice.

Ava took a deep breath, pressed the butt of the shotgun to her shoulder, and stood up, cocking the weapon so that she had their attention. All eyes in the bar flickered to her, and that was exactly what she needed. With calm and collected movements, she stepped back out from behind the bar and kept the weapon trained on them. She wouldn't look away for a second. If they wanted to mess with this bar, then they would have to mess with a Fringer too.

"How about you boys pack your shit and crawl back into whatever hole it was you slunk out of," Ava said ferociously.

She walked slowly forward. The trick to pulling a move like this was to let them know that you were dangerous and wouldn't be intimidated. This situation didn't scare her at all as this was just another day back home. Stupid men throwing their weight around, hoping to get their own way.

"Aww, darling, how about you get back behind that bar and pour me a drink," the lead man sneered. Without hesitation, Ava lowered the barrel and shot the shell into the floor at his feet. There was an almighty shout as a few of the buckshot buried themselves into his foot. She snapped the weapon straight up to cover the rest of the crowd.

"Pour it yourself," Ava said as the guy dropped to the floor, clutching his foot. "Now where were we? Oh, yeah, get out of here?"

Ava felt a little smug. For the first time since she had crossed the wall, she felt like she held some power. She felt like the person that she was supposed to be. Not some weak ass female who was hiding from a world she didn't know, or a woman who pined over a man even though she had done that only five minutes ago. Well, no more. She was Ava, and that was who she was going to be.

"You just couldn't stay away, could you?" came Glass' voice from the doorway.

Ava's head snapped around to see Glass standing in the back doorway behind the bar. She held a pistol pointed directly at her. Ava's heart started pounding faster. There was no way she could move this shotgun and fire before Glass could pull the trigger.

"Glass, put the gun down," Jacques said as he slowly got to his feet with his hands raised.

"Oh, you're on her side? Is that how it's going to be?" Glass said, hate dripping from her voice. "That's it, after all those years, you replace me?"

"You left. You fucked off," Jacques said, the anger so obvious in his tone.

"Well, I'm back now. We can forget all the shit that happened," Glass said. There was an odd note to her voice, and her head tilted slightly to the side. There was something about her jerky movement that was very disconcerting. Ava gripped the shotgun tighter as she prepared to shoot if she needed to. "I'm back for you and for this bar. We can go back to how things used to be. Just you and me."

"Glass, I'm not interested. I'm with Ava now, and I'm happy," Jacques said. The words made Ava's heart leap with a giddy happiness, but the effect on Glass was obvious, and now was not the time. The other woman's face turned a deep red. Ava saw her re-grip the pistol. Her hands were shaking with poorly suppressed fury.

"Well, if I kill her then you'll have to have me," Glass said with a maniacal grin.

Everything seemed to go in slow motion. Even from this distance, she saw Glass' finger twitch, and heard the explosive sound of the gun echo through the room. Ava shut her eyes, waiting to feel the harsh pain of the bullet tearing into her skin. Moments later, when nothing came, she opened her eyes. A body was blocking her. Hamish. His large form dropped to his knees, and his hand clutched a wound on his chest. What the hell had he done?

Chapter Eighteen

The second that Glass had emerged from that back room, Jacques knew that everything was going to go to shit. He just sensed it. Where Glass seemed to go, trouble always seemed to follow her, and now everything about her was wrong. She wasn't the girl that he'd fallen in love with all those years ago. She was a psychotic mess that hid in her pretty physical shell. He'd never expected her to take that shot.

The second the trigger was pulled, he felt his world crumbling down. He was going to lose Ava, and he wasn't close enough to do anything. Then Hamish threw himself forward, the old man's body taking the lethal shot that had been intended for Ava. He hadn't expected Hamish to be the one taken, but the emotional impact still hit him like a hammer blow.

Jacques ran to Hamish's side and dropped to his knees. Blood was pouring from the bullet hole in Hamish's chest, and his face was quickly turning pale as the puddle of blood grew on the floor. Jacques panicked and pressed his hand on the wound. That's what you did to stop the bleeding, right? His breath was coming faster and faster.

"Hey…it's gonna be alright," Hamish said as he grabbed Jacques' wrist. His voice was pained and weak, and Jacques didn't like that.

"We'll get an ambulance; you'll be fine," Jacques said in a panicked tone.

"We both know it's too late," Hamish said. A cough came from him which made his entire body shake. Blood seeped from the corners of his mouth.

"No…no…it can't be," Jacques said. Hamish was the closest thing to a father figure that he'd ever had. The man had truly cared for him every fucking day, even when he was being a complete asshole. Hamish's hand grabbed for Jacques' lapel and pulled him in close, Hamish's lips close to his ear.

"You marry Ava, you put a bunch of damn babies in her, and you lead a good fucking life, you hear me?" Hamish said in a quiet tone. Jacques felt his throat closing as tears welled up in the corners of his eyes. "Promise me."

"I need you," Jacques whispered so only Hamish could hear. In this moment, he felt like a child. He felt the smallest he had ever been.

"Promise me," Hamish repeated.

"I promise," Jacques said back. "I promise."

"You're a good kid," Hamish said.

The grip on his jacket loosened as Hamish seemed to lose his strength. He was as white as a sheet, and his breathing was growing steadily slower. Jacques stared at him, praying someone would do something, that a miracle would happen, but nothing came. He watched as moments later, his chest stilled.

Jacques couldn't quite believe what had just happened. Anger started burning deep down inside him, cutting through the sadness until it filled every part of him. There was never a time in his life that he'd felt like he did in that moment.

He looked up from Hamish's body, and his eyes instantly connected with Glass'. The look of shock and horror on her face was worlds away from the psycho who had taken the shot. Not that that mattered to him. Any semblance of care or concern for her had been lost the second she pulled the trigger.

He stood straight up. Ava had been standing over them still holding the shotgun, defending both him and Hamish. Anger and pain was pasted on her face. Hamish had been her friend, too. She glanced to Jacques before her eyes jumped around the room, surveying the situation.

"Get out of this bar," Jacques said, his voice low and dangerous. He just wanted Glass and her lackeys out of the bar. He needed them to leave before he did something that he would come to regret.

"Jacques. I didn't mean it. I meant to kill her," Glass said. The hardass seemed completely lost now, the voice that of the naive girl that he first met coming from the mouth of a killer. Only moments ago, he thought he could save her, but now she had killed her own father, there was no chance. As she edged closer to him, she placed her pistol on the bar. It seemed like she was trying to look at the body of her father. He was sure that he could see a hint of tears in her eyes, but he didn't trust how true they were.

The movement was so quick that Jacques didn't see it coming, and neither did Ava. A knife was suddenly in Glass' hand, and in one quick movement, she buried the weapon in Ava's side. There was a cry of pain from Ava. Jacques went to grab Glass, but he was restrained from behind before he could reach her.

"Defend the Casket!" came a cry from somewhere in the room.

That was when everything descended into madness. The mercs who had been watching intently from around the room went on the offensive, causing the gangers to spread and start fighting back. Jacques didn't care about them. All he cared about was getting to Ava; he had to know if she was alright. He couldn't lose her and Hamish in the same day. He just needed to make sure she was still standing, but a mass of people were fighting between them. He caught glimpses of Glass, but he couldn't see Ava. A pit of sickness rolled in his stomach. He had to find her.

His emotions seemed to take hold, allowing him a burst of strength. He flung his arms back, throwing the lead guy off him. He didn't try to fight. He focused on pushing his way through the mass of people. He was expecting to see her on the ground lying next to Hamish, but there she was fighting Glass hand to hand. The look of anger on her face was feral. Glass' move had awoken the fighter in her, and Jacques suspected Glass would come to regret that. He didn't get the chance to watch the fight progress as the lead ganger was coming back for him. Knowing that she was at least able to defend herself fueled him. Ava was from the The Fringe, and her harsh life had prepared her for these kinds of situations. If he was going to stand by her side, he needed to show he was every bit as capable at defending himself as she was. Now he was glad that Lucy had dragged him to some of Zane's self-defense classes.

Jacques blocked the first swing. A heavy kick connected with his shin as the guy tried to take him down, but there was no way that he was going to let that happen. This was his fight, and he was going to win it. He kept blocking and waited for an opening to attack. It came quickly, as his opponent dropped his guard every time he hit with his left. On the next attack, Jacques took advantage of the weakness, landing several heavy blows and forcing the guy backwards.

There was fighting everywhere. It seemed like the mercs who used this joint felt a connection with it just as he had. It was a home for those who didn't have one, and the misfits it took in were eager to defend it. He was just glad that guns weren't being used. The sound would bring the security, and he didn't want their help. This was their place to protect.

*****

The second that silver blade had connected with her side, Ava had sworn at herself. How could she not be expecting some underhand shit from that woman? The knife had skimmed her ribs and, luckily, buried somewhere in the loose jumper she wore rather than her flesh. That was good. It was a slight injury that she could fight through, and she was going to fight. This bitch had got the better of her once, and that wasn't going to happen again.

Glass had used her trick card. That stupid augmentation that allowed her speed. Ava couldn't keep up with that, but she could fight smarter now that she knew what to expect, and that was what she was going to do. Glass was coming at her with a ferocity that she hadn't used last time. It seemed like losing Jacques to her, or the killing of her father, or both, had really brought out the psychotic killer within her.

"You're going to die, bitch," Ava snarled.

She didn't let Glass get on a roll and went on the attack. A good offense was the best defense in her books. The more you pushed the enemy, the harder it would be for them to attack back. Glass would know what it felt like for every inch of you to hurt. Ava would make sure of that.

Ava focused on Glass' left side. She needed to avoid hitting that metal arm, else even a block could break her hand, and she couldn't afford that right now. A kick to Glass' knee caused her to stumble backwards. Ava used the distraction to bring a fist up into her ribs, and she was pretty damn sure she felt a rib break.

The battle around her faded to the background. Glass was all she saw. She lunged, a perfect hit connecting with her face, and a crunch as her nose pasted across her face. *An eye for an eye*, Ava thought. Both of Glass' hands came up in response, grabbing her face. Blood poured down her chin. She spat and peered through her fingers; that look of anger was back again.

"Aww, did that hurt?" Ava said mockingly.

She was pushing Glass to use that fucking enhancement. Ava had spent the combat pushing her into a good location where speed wasn't going to matter. Ava had never been so determined in her life. This fight wasn't about Jacques; it was about getting revenge for the first attack. There was no way she could live without getting her own back after what had happened.

"You know how this went the first time. Back down," Glass said, her voice distorted from the broken nose.

"I don't think you have it in you to beat me again," Ava said. She was doing everything she could to rile her up. "I think you won by fluke last time."

"Oh, bitch, you have no idea," Glass responded.

As expected, she had taken the bait. Ava saw the moment the augmentation kicked in. There was a buzz to her, her pupils widened, and her gaze darted erratically around the room. She was ready. Glass lost no more time before going on the offensive. The first attack was with that big, heavy arm. Expecting the movement, Ava dodged left. The next attack was a kick; expecting it, Ava dodged backwards.

Glass lunged forward, the attack falling short as she tripped a few broken barstools, and she went down, hitting the floor hard. The augment may make her faster, but it didn't help if she didn't watch her surroundings. Ava had moved her so the barstool was basically under her feet. The plan had worked, and Glass was on the ground. Ava wasted no time as she dropped to the floor and pinned her.

"You don't fuck with Fringers," she said smugly.

Chapter Nineteen

Lucinda hadn't expected this. Any of this. If anything was going to go wrong, she had expected it to happen at the club. When things had gone so smoothly, she had really thought they were out of the woods. There was no way she expected the gang to track them back here. No one had followed them in the car, and she wondered how they knew Glass had been brought here. Not that it mattered in this moment.

Throughout the conversation, Zane had been tense. One hand had stayed around his beer while the other held Caspian's shoulder under the table. It seemed like he was holding himself back from getting involved. It must be a real blast from the past for him. His mouth was a grim line and his jaw tense as he watched the interaction. Even Caspian was ready to interfere. From her limited view, she could see that he was leaned forward on his knees, ready to throw himself forward.

That was proven the second the fight kicked off. Caspian was out from under the table and Zane out of his seat within seconds. The two men acted like a wall of muscle protecting her from the fray before them. There was a glance between them before they nodded to each other, an identical look of determination on their faces.

There was so much activity in the bar it was hard to keep track of what was going on. At one time, this sort of situation would have scared the hell out of her, and she would have been terrified to the point of hiding until it was over. But since she had begun training with Zane, she felt a lot more confident in her own abilities. Her main issue now was what to do. She tracked the combat, trying to figure where she would best be of help.

"Luce, duck," Caspian said. She followed his direction as something came flying in her direction. As she looked back up, Caspian had grabbed a guy and slammed him to the floor, grasping his throat. "Stay safe."

She wasn't insulted that Caspian was warning her to stay clear of the fight. She didn't exactly have the physical prowess that they did. The skills she had weren't brawling, they were self-defense, to take someone down so she could run or get help. A full on barroom brawl wasn't something she had planned for. She'd even left her Taser in Hamish's borrowed car.

Jacques was in combat with the lead guy, and he seemed to be handling the fight well. They were meeting each other blow for blow. Ava was off to the side fighting with Glass. The two women's fight seemed more brutal than any other combat in the room. Ava had a point to prove, and the girl was proving it. Glass seemed to be giving no quarter, either.

Her eyes drifted back to Zane and Caspian. The brothers were fighting back to back, each of them covered by the other. Their moves seemed to flow together like a perfectly choreographed dance. They must have fought together so much that they had become the perfect unit.

That's when a realization hit her. It was the complete worst time, but you couldn't help when the life-changing epiphanies came to you. Even though the brothers fought, and those fights were violent and worrying, it had led to a bond that was deeper than anything she'd ever seen. Years of living in The Fringe and fighting for their lives had created something that couldn't be broken. Sure, their tempers got the better of them, and they took it out on each other, but when something important came along, they could put that to one side and stand together against anything.

She had spent the last couple of weeks watching the family, picking them apart and trying to find a reason why she couldn't move in. The reason? She was scared. She was scared by how much she cared about Zane and the family. She was scared that one day she would come home to find them gone without a trace. It had taken her so long to get over the disappearance of her parents, and twelve years later, it still killed her that she had never found them.

She didn't really care that Zane and Caspian got into fights, or that Sawyer could possibly steal her stuff. She didn't care that the twins were always in trouble at school, or the fact that Blair was already behind in her classes. Deep down, she was worried that they would all go away. and she would be left alone again.

The family's bond was so deep that they would protect each other to the end of the world and further if they needed to. That was what she needed. She needed that kind of fire in her life. For so many years, she had been looking for a place where she fit in. Somewhere she could belong. This was it. She belonged with Zane and his family. She couldn't sit here trying to desperately protect her heart. She needed to jump in two feet first and give this relationship everything she had.

Feeling invigorated, she jumped from beneath the booth. As Caspian dodged a punch from his assailant, Lucinda brought her fist up, catching the man in the solar plexus. He expelled a huge lungful of air as he staggered backwards.

"Zane, I'm gonna move in with you," Lucinda said.

"You made that decision right now?" Zane asked, sounding confused. He threw a kick at his opponent and forced him away.

"Yeah, I know I've been acting weird, but if it's okay with you, we'll talk later," she said. Even in the midst of combat, she couldn't fight the smile that was on her face.

"I'm down for that. Now go help Ava," Zane said as he nodded in the bar's direction.

"On it," Lucinda said. She went to move, but stopped to glance at Zane. "I love you."

"I love you, too," Zane said as he grabbed the next assailant and threw him to the ground.

With that image in her mind, she turned and made her way across the bar. She dodged past the bouts of combat or assisted as she went. None of them seemed to be using knives or any weapons, which meant they weren't fighting to kill. That was something she was glad of. The likeliness of someone else getting killed was low.

Glass was on the floor by the time Lucinda got there. The woman had a look of shock on her face as Ava pinned her to the hardwood floor. The feral look on the Fringer's face was disconcerting. The look didn't suit her pretty features.

"How can I help?" Lucinda asked.

"Rope, string…fucking scarves. Anything I can restrain her with," Ava shouted to her.

Lucinda looked around the bar. There was far too much fighting going on for her to be able to find anything. She threw herself over the bar and decided to head for the back rooms, hoping to find something there.

There was a crash behind her as a body came flying over the bar. There was a shattering of glass as the person broke a shelf and a load of glasses. She looked around to find Jacques lying in the mess. She quickly ran to check on him.

"Jacques, are you okay?" she asked, the worry almost suffocating.

"Yeah, yeah," he said, clutching his chest as he got to his feet. "I need a favor."

"What?" she asked.

"I need you to distract the guy I was fighting. I have a way to end this," Jacques said.

"Yeah, I can do that, but you need to get Ava a rope," she said. Even at the thought, her heart started beating a little a faster. She was already telling herself that she could do this, and mentally running through all of the moves that Zane had taught her over the year.

She stood up, surveying the bar to find her opponent. He was already heading this way. Probably looking for the guy he threw into the drinks cabinet. There was blood pooling from his nose, and there was a pissed off look plastered over his face. Oh, she was no way ready for this, but she was going to do this. No being the pretty little girl anymore.

"Oh, Zane's augmented leg, Seattle grade augment, right?" Jacques asked.

"Yeah," she responded, a little confused. When she glanced around to ask him why, he was already gone. She shook her head, turned back to her assailant, and jumped on the bar. Time to fight.

*****

The plan had come to Jacques when that augmented hand had connected with his cheek. He wasn't a fighter, not really. He knew enough to get out of a scrap, but in a prolonged fight, there was little chance that he would win. That's why he had to rely on his brain. As he ran into the back room, he started raiding the storage shelves.

When he was first homeless, he'd found a garage full of old outdated electrical devices that hadn't been used in decades. Using the old fashioned handbooks, he'd taught himself all about electronics and how they worked. There was one piece of tech that could really help him out here. An EMP. If he could create a strong enough electromagnetic pulse, then he stood a chance of knocking out the gangers who were flooding the bar.

From the research he'd done on the Chrome Razors, he knew a lot of their augmentics would be black market or just poor quality. Augmentics like Zane's leg that came from legitimate Seattle sources would come with EMP shielding, but the second rate stuff, no way. EMP shielding was expensive to produce and install. All he needed to do was find suitable parts. Luckily, Hamish never threw anything away which might come in handy.

He started dragging old machines off the shelf and tearing them apart. He could hear the fight that was raging in the next room. He had no idea what side was winning, but things didn't seem to be calming at all. If anything, it was starting to sound worse.

Now he wished he hadn't taken the job from Hamish. If he'd just left her alone, then none of this would have happened. Hamish wouldn't be dead, Ava wouldn't be hurt, and the bar he loved wouldn't be under siege. No, he couldn't start thinking about that; he needed to focus on the job ahead. There would be plenty of time to mourn Hamish when other lives weren't in danger.

It only took a few minutes to put the device together. The device was small, but it should cover the entire bar area; if not, then it would knock a few of them offline long enough to give the Casket's people the upper hand. He was going to have to activate it and run, though. The augmented eyes he had were second hand and poor quality. There was no way that they would survive an EMP. All he had to do was set the thing on the bar, hit the button for it to activate, and then he had about ten seconds to get to the alley out the back. Easy.

With the device in hand, he slipped back into the bar.

*****

Ava didn't know how long she had been pinning Glass, but she did know that her arms were starting to hurt from restraining that augmented arm. She didn't know how long she could hold it. Lucinda had gone for rope but had ended up fighting. Now she was waiting on Jacques, and he was taking his fucking time. She could feel the burn in her biceps as Glass was trying to push her off. There was no way she was losing to this bitch again.

She glanced to the door behind the bar just in time to see Jacques walking out. There was an instant relief in her chest. That was until she noticed he wasn't carrying any rope, just…she didn't even know what he was carrying.

Recycled Lives

Suddenly, Glass threw her hand out. Ava couldn't maintain her grip, and Glass broke free. Fuck! There was no way that she was going to trick Glass again. She had to think of another way to take her down. Ava went to throw herself out of the way so Glass couldn't catch her, but she was too slow. Glass caught her wrist in the metal hand. Her grip was quickly getting tighter and tighter, threatening to shatter the bone.

Ava bit her lip, fighting against the pain of the hold. There was no way she was going to gasp; she didn't need to give Glass the satisfaction of knowing how much damage she was doing. She wanted to think her way out of this, but she couldn't think past the pain that was radiating from her crushed limb.

She wanted to yell out for Jacques to help, but her pride was holding her back. She could do this herself; that's how things had always been. But that wasn't how things should be anymore, should they? What the fuck was Jacques doing over there? Why the fuck wasn't he helping anyone?

*****

As Jacques went to activate the EMP, the thing had started to fall it apart in his hand. He was currently the only thing that was holding it together. He needed more time to fix the thing. It would only take maybe two minutes. He glanced up to the room and was instantly concerned when Glass wasn't still pinned on the floor. The two women were fighting again. He hoped that Ava would win, but it was obvious that she was struggling, and that concerned him.

A bead of sweat dripped down his forehead as he fumbled through his tool kit, trying desperately to fix the EMP. Every time he fixed it, it seemed that something else was breaking. He wanted to scream and shout, but that wasn't going to help him right now. What he needed was to focus on the job at hand. Not the combat.

He glanced up again. Lucinda was still going blow for blow with his assailant, and she was holding her own, but the blood on her face showed she wasn't going uninjured in the process. Fuck! It was all going to shit. This had seemed like a good idea, but as usual, things were falling apart around him. He was about to give up on the whole EMP idea when he glanced over to see that Glass had Ava in a hold.

The whole world seemed to slow down as a glint of silver appeared in Glass' flesh hand. It was the knife from earlier. There was no way that he was going to be able to cross that distance in time, and if he shot with his gun, he had more of a chance of hitting Ava than Glass. He looked down at the device in his hand. He only had once choice.

"Glass, don't do this," Jacques shouted. Her head snapped around to him; a smug look covered her pretty face.

"This is all her fault. If it wasn't for her, Dad would still be alive," Glass said. There was no sense of sadness in her tone. Her words said that she cared, but her voice and her face didn't give off any of those signs. She was saying what he needed to hear; he was sure of it.

"No, Glass. It's your fault. This is all your fault," Jacques said. Whatever he had done in the past may have influenced who she was, but it was her choice to act on it. He was done taking responsibility for other people's actions. The hand gripping the knife started to lower. He was getting through to her. "You can stop this; no one else needs to die."

"No...no...it's hers," Glass said with a waver in her tone. Her brows lowered as she tried to fight whatever was going on in her own head. She paused with a look of determination on her face. "She has to die."

In a quick movement, Glass brought the knife up. His time was up. He hit the button on the EMP. There was an explosion of electricity from his hand and a surge of static in the air. There were cries and the sounds of thuds.

He was confused for a second. He could still see the bar. He could still see Glass holding Ava. Had the EMP failed? That's when he realized the final imprint of the scene had been imprinted on his augmented eyes. How long it would last, he didn't know, but that image was there, front and center. The look on Glass' face as she felt like she had her vengeance, and Ava's face as she thought she was going to die.

His heart started to beat fast in his chest. He was blind. Completely and utterly blind. There was still a cacophony of noise in the bar. It didn't sound like fighting, but he couldn't work out what was going on. He dropped the remnants of the EMP and stumbled forward grabbing the edge of the bar for support. He needed to know what had happened. He was starting to panic that he'd been too late.

"Ava…Ava…are you okay?" Jacques shouted.

"Yeah. I'm okay," was her flustered response. He felt an impact on the other side of the bar and flinched, ready to jump away.

"I…I can't see," he stuttered. Right now, he was actually scared, something he hadn't felt for a long time. He felt hands grab both of his and squeeze slightly.

"What was that?" she asked, her breath coming fast and heavy as she seemed to be trying to catch it.

"A small EMP. It should have knocked out the augmentics. Did it work?" he asked, panic about to overtake him. He had to assume it did; how else would she be standing here?

"Yeah. Most just collapsed. Some are still conscious, but their augmentics have stopped working," Ava said.

Relief flooded him. It had worked, they were safe, and the fight was over. Well, kind of. He still had to figure out what he was going to do with Glass. Hamish was the only one able to corral her, and now he was dead. All those feelings that he'd been suppressing were starting to bubble to the surface. He forced himself to swallow. This still wasn't the time for that.

"Glass. What happened to her?" Jacques asked.

"She…she got away," Ava said. His stomach dropped. No! How the hell could she have gotten away?

"We'll get her. You'll be safe, I promise," he said quickly.

"I doubt the bitch is coming back after that," Ava said with a forced chuckle. "Now sit down before you hurt yourself. I need to help the others, okay?"

Her lips pressed against his for just a second before she pulled away from him. He felt completely lost and useless. He wanted to help, but he couldn't even fucking see. He kept blinking, wanting to clear the image that was burned into his eyes. But no matter what he did, it was there. Was this the image he was stuck with for the rest of his days? He would welcome the endless darkness right now.

Chapter Twenty

Ava stood holding Jacques' hand as she lied to his face. Glass hadn't gotten away; she lay on the floor not far away. Her face was pale and quickly taking on a gray hue. She wasn't breathing; she was dead. The second that static had erupted in the air, something had happened to her. Her arm had gone limp, then her body had started to tremble before she dropped to the floor in seizure. When she stopped jerking, that was it.

When he'd asked about her, she wanted to tell him the truth, but that would tear him apart. The last time he had ended up killing someone, it had caused such damage that if he found out that he had killed someone he had once loved so much, then it would completely tear him apart. She wasn't willing to let that happen to him.

As she pulled away, she looked into those white eyes. It was ironic because he'd told her he used the blind eyes as decoys for many years, but now he was actually blind. Foreshadowing much? She wanted to focus on him, but she needed to act quickly if she was going to get rid of Glass' body. If this was The Fringe, she would have just dragged her to the outskirts and buried her. In Seattle, things were very different.

Everyone was a little frantic with what had happened, so no one was looking her way. The mercs were picking themselves up and dusting themselves off while the gangers were dragging themselves out of there, licking their wounds. Before anyone noticed, she quickly grabbed Glass' body and lifted her into her arms before slipping her way into the back room. She ditched the body on her old bed, grabbed a sheet, and wrapped the body up in it before heading back to the bar, locking the door to her room in the process. If anyone asked where she had gone, she would lie her fucking ass off. When you loved someone, you protected them. Wait, had she just thought that? Yes, she had. She loved him. He was the first guy to have treated her as more than a piece of meat, and she was willing to protect him. Okay, she needed off this train of thought.

Jacques was sitting there behind the bar, and Lucinda was with him, which would buy her a little more time.

In her time as a bartender here, she had gotten to know the usual mercs. Each of them had different sets of skills, and right now, she needed one in particular—body removal. She knew that one of the lead guys for it had been in the bar today, and for the right price, he would help her out.

He was currently seated by the door. Sherrie had just served him a drink. All those who had fought were being given a drink on the house. She glanced around, making sure no one was focused on her, and when she was satisfied, she slipped herself into the seat opposite.

"You alright?" he grunted as he pulled back a gauze pad to check a gash on his hand.

"Yeah. I'm in need of your services," she whispered. "I have a body I need you to get rid of."

The man glanced around the bar as if searching for the body. He zeroed in on Hamish for a moment before he looked back to her and narrowed his brow. Her heart was thudding away. If this guy didn't help her, then she only had a few other options. The last thing she needed was to lose her freedom before she even started her life here in Seattle because she didn't dispose of her man's ex-girlfriend's body properly.

"Not Hamish. Glass bit the big one, and I need her to disappear before anyone notices," Ava explained in a low voice. There was no point lying; as soon as he saw the body, he was going to know her. Pretty much all the mercs did.

"It's gonna cost you," he said.

When he reeled off the number, she inwardly cringed. It was going to cost her every penny that she had saved for her new apartment and the materials for her business. It was her fresh start disappearing down the drain. More money she could earn, but there was no other way to protect Jacques. She offered him her hand, and when he accepted it, she transferred all the money his way.

"The body is in the back room; here's the key," she said, handing it over. "Needs to be gone ASAP."

The merc nodded before downing the rest of his drink. Then he was on his feet and on his way. One of the perks of working in the merc bar was that it was easy to get in touch with any illegal services you needed. With that issue dealt with, she needed to go and see Jacques.

He wasn't behind the bar anymore. Now he was knelt at Hamish's side. Lucinda stood not far away just watching over Jacques. Ava went to his side and knelt down, and she placed a hand on his shoulder. He flinched.

"It's me," she said, and his shoulders instantly relaxed. "Are you okay?"

Jacques went silent for a moment. His eyebrows creased, and his mouth twitched as if he was trying to conjure up some words but was failing miserably. She sighed a little. At least she wasn't the only person who was feeling this way. Not that she had ever been good with words, but right now, she couldn't even start to think how to put her feelings into words.

"He was the only parent I ever had," Jacques said, swallowing hard.

Ava had no idea what to say, so instead, she wrapped an arm around his shoulders and pulled him against her. He came willingly. She tried to remember what it was like when her own mother died. What was sad was there was no real emotion. Death was such a normal part of life in The Fringe it was almost expected. When she looked at Hamish, though, she felt a pang of sadness, which was something that she hadn't expected.

"He helped me so much. I never had the chance to repay him," Ava said. When she had arrived here, she had nothing. He had helped her get on her feet.

He brought her clothes, a gauntlet, even an ID chip. He had never really asked for anything; all he had wanted was help in the bar from time to time.

"He wouldn't have wanted a repayment. When he found someone he cared about, he just wanted to help them," Jacques said sadly.

"Look, let's get you home, okay?" Ava said. She really just wanted to get him away from this place, even for just half an hour. "We'll get showered, sort your injuries out. Then we'll sort out what to do next, okay?"

It was selfish, but she wanted him to herself. Everything that needed to be done for the bar right now had been done. A coroner was coming for the body, probably the security, too, but Sherrie and Keith would cover that. They had been briefed on how to lie to the officers by some of the bar's more experience patrons. She wanted to be away from the eyes of all the mercs and from his friends. Not just that, but she knew he needed to be away before he could process his emotions properly. She stood up and assisted him to his feet. Once again, he came willingly.

No one asked any questions as they headed for the door. Her gauntlet had been fried in the EMP. Luckily, the ID chips were shielded, so she flagged down the first cab that passed them. There was no conversation as they made their way across the city. There was a lot to process with everything that had happened today. When the cab stopped outside of Jacques apartment, she paid the fare and led him up the stairs into his apartment.

They settled together on the couch. Ava released a slight sigh. She had been trying to figure where everything had gone wrong, but then at the end of the day, it didn't really matter. Now it was just about picking up the pieces. Jacques was just sat there with his hands clutched tightly together. All she could focus on was his bloody knuckles. She fetched the iodine from the medicine cabinet and sat on the floor before him. She took his hand.

"This is going to sting," she said.

She gently jabbed iodine on the broken skin of his knuckles. His body stiffened with each touch, and once she was done, she brought his hand to her lips and kissed each one gently. She took a moment to lift her top, dabbing a bit of the iodine on the cut on her side before stepping up and taking his hand, bringing him to his feet.

"Do you want to take a shower?" she asked.

"With you?" he asked.

"If that's what you want," she said.

"If I ever say no to that, then I am ill as hell," he said with a slight smirk.

Ava couldn't help the small smile as he took her hand. They made their way into the bathroom. They stripped each other slowly. Even with his blindness, Jacques had no issue taking her clothes off. When they stepped under the water, a calming sense overtook her, like everything that happened was being washed away and was replaced by his touch. A touch that for the first time in her life felt right. A touch she didn't resent but, instead, encouraged.

"I love you," he whispered.

"And I you," she replied, the admittance bringing a wave of euphoria from within.

After what felt like hours, she stepped from beneath the spray, her legs weak and her head sated. She could live in that moment for the rest of her days. The moment that she felt like a person, not an object. The time a person showed her what a loving touch was. A time that she would remember for the rest of her days.

Epilogue

Lucinda grabbed the final box off the back of the moving van and carried it into the house. After the fight in the Oaken Casket, Lucinda had realized a few things about herself that she hadn't been expecting. One of them being that she could kick ass now, and the other being that whatever happened in life, she wanted Zane by her side. Even with the fights between them, the sticky fingers, and the endless school meetings, she wanted to be part of his family.

When they had gotten back from the Oaken Casket, they had all been beaten, bloody, and bruised. Sawyer hadn't hesitated to get out the first aid kit and go about fixing their injuries. Apparently, when they had lived in The Fringe, she had been a little nurse for the family and was more than accustomed to cleaning up her brothers after a fray.

She had slid into bed with Zane at the end of the day, and she had told him that she wanted to live here. More than that, though, she wanted to be a part of his family and everything that entailed. Most people would think she was moving too fast, but when it felt right, you just had to go for it. Too much of her life up to this point had been carefully planned. This was where she let her heart take over, but her head agreed that she had made the best choice for herself.

"Is that the last one?" Zane asked as he met her by the front door.

"Yeah, just this one, and I'm all moved in. I handed my keys to my old place over on the way out. I officially live here now," she said with a smile.

"We are glad to have you here," Zane said as he wrapped an arm around her waist and pulled her in for a kiss.

"Where does this one go?" Caspian asked as he took one of the boxes from inside the door.

"What does it say on the box?" she asked.

"Uhh…kitchen," he said. He poked his tongue out at her and headed through to the kitchen. She chuckled before grabbing another box.

When the kids came home from school, she hoped to have all of her stuff moved in, and with Zane, Dare, and Caspian's help, she doubted that would be a problem. She looked around the living area. Even though it was so different from when she had grown up, she could still see what it used to be. She could see her Mom in the kitchen cooking dinner, and Dad flicking through the channels looking for something to watch.

It had taken one day for her entire life to come crumbling down around her, and to this day, she didn't know what had happened to her parents. She doubted she ever would. Now she realized it was time to put that behind her. No amount of wishing would bring her parents back to her, but here she had the family that she had so desperately craved. She had a group of people who cared about her and she knew would have her back. In this world, that was all that mattered.

Even with all the darkness in her past, she was now looking forward, and all she could think was that her future felt a whole lot brighter. Even if she had given up any sense of privacy she could have. She wouldn't give this family up for anything. She thought about that picture that Blair had drawn last week, and that brought a smile to her face.

"We should get Blair a chocolate fountain for her birthday. I think she'd like that," she said to Zane as he came up to grab another box. He snorted.

"I don't doubt it. She's a sweet fiend," Zane said before he laughed. He turned away and took a step before he turned to look at her again.

"Lucy, thank you," he said without an explanation.

"Thank you for what?" she asked.

"For being you. You're more than I could have ever hoped for," he said.

The gesture made her swell with happiness. After leaving the children's home, she couldn't really imagine any happy future for herself. Everything seemed so bleak and hopeless. Now here she stood in her family home with a new family at her side. With these guys, she felt more powerful than ever, like she could take on the world. There wasn't anything that she would change.

Yasmin Hawken

*****

Ava had spent the last few days helping the staff at the Oaken Casket clean up the bar and come to terms with the loss of Hamish. The physical damage to the bar was minimal; the few broken barstools and smashed glasses could be easily replaced. Hamish not so much. Everyone was still reeling from the shock of it all. Seattle Security's investigation had been wrapped up pretty swiftly. The staff had stuck to the half-truth that the gangers came looking for trouble, and Hamish was a victim of the cross fire, and omitted the fact that kidnapping Glass had provoked the attack in the first place. The number of dead gangers in the bar had confirmed this story, and the officers had written the incident off as another example of gang violence in the area.

The Casket was pretty quiet tonight with only the most stubborn regulars in sight. The Security presence over the last few days had kept most of the clients away, but they would be back once they were sure the Security interest in the bar had quietened down. Ava had clocked out early and allowed herself some time to sort her things out. With both Hamish and Glass dead, the future of the Casket was uncertain, and she wanted to make sure all her shit was ready to go if the shit hit the fan. She was just sorting through the pile of fabrics she had recently bought when there was a knock on the door. She crossed the room to see who her unexpected guest was. On the other side of the door stood India wearing Ava's jacket.

"Hey, how you holding up?" India asked.

"I'm doing okay, thanks. Are you okay?" Ava replied.

"Yeah, I'm cool. Can I come in?" India said, indicating Ava's room. Ava stepped back from the doorway and gestured inside. India entered and settled herself onto the center of Ava's bed.

"So… What's up?" Ava said.

"Well, it's like this. I was at the party and Candice Miller came up to me and was like 'OMG when did you get that outfit? I need one' and I was like 'It's from an exclusive boutique', and now she totally wants some of her own, and because she wants it, so does everyone else in the class. So can I give out your message to them to get some custom stuff cos they are going crazy for it and I'm the most popular girl in school right now?" India said. Ava was pretty sure the girl had said the whole thing in one breath.

She blinked, a little bewildered. India talked at a million miles a minute, and her brain was still trying to catch up with all the information that India had spouted at her. She hadn't thought the outfit would have been that popular, especially considering it was something she just threw together in twenty minutes. If the kids were impressed by something so simple, she could be making money hand over fist before she knew it. That was if the kids had any money to spend.

"Not personal messenger, no, but I'll set up something so they can send requests. It not going to be free, though, so they better be able to pay properly," Ava said sternly. She didn't want India getting it into her head that Ava was her private tailor.

The girl was sweet but also likely to push her luck as far as she could.

"Of course they can pay. Candice has her own credit account that her dad gave her for her birthday, and everyone gets some allowance from their parents for stuff." India scoffed at her.

It was strange for Ava to imagine a world where even the children had enough money to spend it on whatever they wanted. In The Fringe, a child accepted what they were given and hoped their parents kept a roof over their heads. Anything else was a bonus.

"As long as they pay, I don't care where it comes from," Ava said, giving the girl a grin. If she could make a little money off India's school friends, she'd have enough to start up her business properly. "Now, you gonna give me back my jacket, or am I gonna have to wrestle it off you?"

India huffed good-naturedly and shrugged the black jacket on to the bed. Suddenly, India's gauntlet started chiming at her. She looked at the caller ID, squealed, and rushed for the door.

"Oh my god! He's calling me. I can't believe it. Chat later, Ava. Bye bye." And with that, India rushed from the room.

Finally alone, Ava settled back into packing her things. At least if she had to move, she had the beginnings of a customer base, and in truth, they were the best kind. People with a little too much money and not enough sense on what to spend it on. Even though her future at the Casket was uncertain, her life was generally looking up. Things with Jacques were going well, and soon, she would be able to make a start on being her own boss. She had come a long way from the trash heaps of The Fringe, and she knew she could only get stronger no matter what was thrown her way.

*****

Jacques had been blind for eight days. They had been the hardest days of his life. Although, he had learned something he'd never expected. He'd learned what it was like to truly trust another human being. Ava had barely left his side in those eight days. She'd made sure that he was safe, and that just made him feel like the luckiest man on Earth. Their nights had been spent cleaning up the Oaken Casket, or rather Ava cleaning and him feeling rather useless, and the days curled up together in bed talking and 'watching' TV.

He'd originally planned to get his eyes replaced with Dr. Silver, but Ava had insisted that he didn't get more black market 'ware. After what he had seen, he had to agree with her. The payback scheme was intense, more than he'd usually pay for anything, but the Network health insurance covered a large portion, which was something he was glad for. At least now he'd be able to rely on these eyes. When he'd opened his new eyes for the first time, it had been her face that he'd been looking at, and it was the best first sight. At least the image of Glass and her was gone, not that he'd ever forget it.

Hamish's funeral had happened only a few days after the brawl. The man wouldn't want to waste time, and so many people had turned out to the funeral that not everyone could fit in the church. He'd never seen such a large group of criminals and runaways that owed that man so much. Things wouldn't be the same without him, and he wasn't sure where he was going to go from here. How did he move forward without Hamish? He'd always looked after Jacques, been there with an answer when he needed it.

It turned out that even after his death, that didn't change. Two days after his funeral, a lawyer had turned up on Jacques' doorstep. What he carried was a document which made the Oaken Casket solely his. A letter included explained how he didn't trust Glass to be the proprietor of the bar and the right person needed to keep the place alive. He'd had Ava read the note aloud, and the overwhelming sense of care and love overcame him every time. It was a responsibility that he saw as an honor, but it wasn't for him. That's why he was at the Casket today.

He pushed the door open and stepped into the familiar setting. The scent of blood still hung in the air, but he suspected that the bar's cologne wouldn't change. Not now. Ava was behind the bar refreshing the bottles of spirits. He smiled a little as he remembered how he'd lost himself within her body this evening before work.

"You're really going to have to wear looser jeans to work," Jacques said as he leaned on the bar.

"And why's that?" she asked as she turned around. She grabbed a beer from the fridge and slid it his way.

"Because if anyone touches that ass, I'm gonna kill them," he said with a smirk.

"Is that a new rule, *Boss?*" she said with a smirk. Even if he tried to enforce that rule on her, there was no way she would listen.

"That's actually what I'm here to talk to you about," Jacques said.

"What's going on Jacques?" she asked. Her brows knitted in confusion.

"I don't want to run the bar. It's not for me. The Network is where I belong, and it suits me so much more," Jacques said.

"Wait, you're giving this place up?" Ava asked as she lowered her voice.

"Kind of. I'm giving you full control, if you want it," he said.

She stopped for a second. The look of confusion on her face as she tried to understand what he was saying was damn cute. He sipped at his beer while he waited for some response from her.

"What do you mean?" she asked.

"I'll still own the bar, but that's it. You run it, and you'll have complete control over it," he said. "You'll never have to work for anyone again. You'll be your own boss."

"Are you serious?" she asked.

"Yeah. You have the bad ass attitude to keep the mercs in line, but I know you'll do the right thing to help those who need it. I'll still be here, but I'll just hover in the background. Oh, and drink for free," he said with a smirk.

"I won't let you down," she said. "Between this and my new business, I'm not going to have time to be bored. You think you can give up all that time with me?"

"As long as I get to curl up with you at the end of the night, I'm happy. You have a right to your own life and to do with it as you please," Jacques said.

The look on her face was one he'd never seen before. If he had to guess, it was somewhere between triumph and contentment. This must have been the look on his face when he realized that she was his, the look that said my life is where it needs to be. But now that he'd helped her out, he had one more question for her.

"What was it that you had to get from Big Boss' house the night we left The Fringe?" he asked. "Sorry, it's been bugging me for months."

A look of confusion briefly flickered over her face before she started to laugh. It was so true and unrefined that he knew she was happy. It was a laugh that couldn't be masked by anything else. He watched her, and the joy on her face brought a smile to his.

"Okay, that was a question I wasn't expecting," she said, wiping tears that had formed in the corners of her eyes.

"Well, you didn't seem forthcoming with the information before, so I thought you'd be more likely now that I've given you a bar," he said.

Recycled Lives

"It wasn't anything huge or special. It was a dress," she said. His eyebrows creased. She had gone back into the house to pick up a dress?

"All of that risk for a dress?" he asked.

"It would seem crazy to most. When I was with the Valkyries, everything you had was theirs, and everything you wore was at their discretion. I had a client once, a woman. I saw her regularly," Ava started.

"Chicks, too, huh? Wild," Jacques said.

"Some did, some didn't, and I did. Well, after a while of…you know…she asked me to meet up outside the brothel. Usually, we weren't meant to meet clients outside of the safety of the brothel, but I decided to take the risk. We went for a drink, laughed, walked the bazaars. I saw the dress; it was so pretty and nothing like what I already wore. She bought it for me. Told me that I deserved to feel beautiful once in a while. When Big Boss kicked me out of the compound, I didn't have the chance to save it, so when I went back with you guys, I took my shot."

"So what happened to her?" Jacques asked.

"I don't know. She just stopped coming one day. I heard on the gossip train that she had died," Ava said with a shrug. "An unfortunate side effect of living in The Fringe."

"I'm sorry, love," Jacques said.

"Don't be. It was a long time ago. I guess I just needed that one part of my past back," she said with a smile. "Anyway, I thought you had a meeting at work?"

"Yeah, I'm on my way there now," he said with a smile.

He finished the rest of his beer before getting to his feet. He leaned in and gave Ava a kiss. There was a wolf whistle from one of the mercs, which Jacques responded to with a playful middle finger. As he left the bar, there was a huge smile on his face.

After what was probably the most traumatic two weeks of his life, things were finally starting to look up. Now he was on his way to see Sinclair. The Oaken Casket could become a good resource for the Network if they could make a deal. A lot of whispers passed through that place, and not just that, but plenty of mercs who would kill for a position that came with health insurance. For the first time in many years, he felt like he could breathe. He had a job, a flat, and a beautiful woman to come home to at the end of the day. For the first time in his life, he felt truly happy.